IN SPIRIT

Another woman came into the bar, her head bowed, her features hidden beneath a broad hat. She looked vaguely familiar but, against the sunshine outside, she was little more than a silhouette, a shadow. Without speaking, she crossed the floor, passed Joaquim and disappeared into the short corridor that led to the washroom.

"It's busy!" shouted Joaquim.

He shrugged his shoulders as Jamie glanced across from the far side of the bar, where he was pouring a glass of cold beer.

"She'll find out soon enough," said Joaquim, almost to himself as he turned back to the sardines, flipping them over with the knife.

They both heard the scream.

Have you read?

Point Horror Unleashed

IN SPIRIT

Nick Turnbull

■SCHOLASTIC

To Judy, Scott, Bonnie and Kerry, with love.
And many thanks to Rosemary and
Armindo José Pereira.
Muito obrigado.

Scholastic Children's Books,
Commonwealth House, 1-19 New Oxford Street,
London WC1A 1NU, UK
a division of Scholastic Ltd
London ~ New York ~ Toronto ~ Sydney ~ Auckland
Mexico City ~ New Delhi ~ Hong Kong

First published in the UK by Scholastic Ltd, 2000

Copyright © Nick Turnbull, 2000

ISBN 0 439 99604 X

Typeset by
Cambrian Typesetters, Frimley, Camberley, Surrey
Printed by Cox and Wyman Ltd, Reading, Berks.

10 9 8 7 6 5 4 3 2 1

The Algarve, Southern Portugal, 1753.

It was hot.

Outside, Fr Alvarez could hear the branches of the pine trees shuffling against each other as the soft breeze, blowing in from the sea, pushed through them. But no breeze now blew inside the soiled, drystone walls of the cottage.

Slowly, the priest wiped the back of his hand across the lines of his forehead, his dark green eyes never leaving the young woman who lay on the floor, her eyes almost closed, her body shivering.

The clothes he stood in stuck to the soft, fattened creases of his body. The simple, stained smock, the thick, dark brown shawl, the creased, leather hood that hung about his head, barely hiding the curling, grey strands of hair that clung limply to his skull.

He bent forward again.

"You must ask for forgiveness. It is so simple."

They had beaten her. Long, thick lines of congealed blood ran across the bare skin of her back. Her lower jaw seemed broken. The disfigured hands meant that they had used the "wolf", the steel press that crushed the fingers of its victim. At least she still had her hands. They had not used the guillotine, a blade that took off the limbs.

The single candle sputtered in the corner of the small room, the smoke drifting from its flame, carrying the bitter scent of animal fat. Outside, the sun was falling behind the distant hills, its deepening red staining the broad sweep of the Portuguese skies.

"Please."

The priest's head was lower now, closer to the woman's face.

"They will be here soon."

Her eyelids flickered open, her face turned towards the rough, damp matting of the floor. The priest knew she had no eyes.

In the distance, he could now hear voices.

He knelt.

"In the name of God. . ."

Suddenly the woman twisted upwards, screaming. The bloodied, disfigured fingers of her hands reaching out for the neck of the priest, her broken nails grinding into the soft, ageing flesh.

The priest's bronze crucifix clattered to the floor. Desperately, he clutched at the woman's arms to pull them away, feeling the pain as her grip tightened on his throat; stifled by the hot, rank smell of her breath as she lifted her mouth towards him, and howling in agony as she bit into his neck, her soiled teeth severing his windpipe and the thick arteries that carried his blood.

She screamed as she now stood, letting the body of the priest slump to the floor. A scream of triumph. Of hate. And then, leaving the twitching body of the man of God, she walked to the door.

She could sense them moving slowly towards her. Their voices low. Their feet shuffling and scratching through the dried grasses and ferns that clung to the dusty soil.

No more than silhouettes. Darkened images that moved against the setting sun. Some carried poles. Others held tall hay-forks, their twin points curling upwards from the long wooden handles like the horns of so many devils.

She didn't move. Leaning against the doorway, her torn clothes falling about her, the blood on her skin dried by the heat of the evening.

She felt them come closer. And then stop.

No one spoke.

Some were seeing her for the first time. Others had followed the hunters as they had dragged her from the woods where she had hidden. Others had listened outside the thick walls of the monastery where the monks had beaten her, far into the night. Some even claimed that she had visited them in their dreams.

But none had watched from their windows as the small cortège had passed by their cottages the following morning: the small cart, holding her body, pulled by the donkey; the donkey led by the priest. The only man to have cared for her soul.

None left their homes, until the monks had come back again. The monks who had pointed the finger. Who had identified the young fisherwoman as one whose body had been possessed by the lobisomen. The monks who had told them what to do, as the sun went down.

It was hot.

The woman's mouth opened slightly. The back of her throat tingling. Her pulse quickening. Her hair thickening.

Throwing back her head, she screamed at the skies. A scream that was followed almost immediately by a harsh, gargling sound as she jerked her head down again and tasted the bile in her mouth, letting it drip from the edges of her lips. Once again she screamed, a godless shriek cutting through the dull, red shadows as she faced the men who stood in front of her, the black hollows where her eyes had once been turned towards them.

The scream stopped. She let her arms fall from the doorway. Hunching slightly, she began to move towards them, a low moaning falling from her broken jaws.

And then, shouting, cursing, terrified, the men threw themselves forwards, hurling the stones that they carried. Raising the poles, only to bring them crashing down upon the woman. Burying them in her writhing, kicking, screaming body.

They shouted. In panic, in excitement, in fear. They wrapped the twines about her body, desperately pulling them under her arms, staining them with her blood, beating her into silence. And then they began to run towards the seashore, dragging her body behind them.

Shouting, shrieking, they ran through the scrubland, down the slope to the cold waters of the Atlantic. Across the sands, the young woman's body carving a twisting furrow, dragged like the blunted blade of a plough by fear-crazed horses.

They reached the waves. Now the sun had disappeared behind the hills. Now the spume from the wave tops flew through the air, carrying the smell of the salt and of the creatures that moved beneath the surface.

They took the woman, bundling her body, touching it with fear and with loathing. Together, the men lifted her and then dropped her into the water, pushing her beneath the waves, holding her head deep beneath them. No longer screaming, no longer shouting. A silence on the edge of the sea, broken only by deep breathing, the sound of gulls flying high above and the soft bursting of bubbles as the last pockets of air left the body of the woman and she died.

They left her body draped over an upturned boat. A small fishing boat, pulled high on to the sands.

In the morning, the sun would dry her, as it dried the octopuses that they pulled from the sea – creatures that climbed into the dark recesses of the small earthen pots that had been left on the sea-bed and from which there was no escape. The captured octopus would be hammered against the rocks at the edge of the beach and left in the glare of the Algarve sun, drying, hardening, before being burnt over the embers of a charcoal fire.

They left her there for three days. Dried by the sun during the day. Blown by the soft winds of the night.

They built the pyre at the edge of the narrow, dusty road that led away from the sea, past the few small white cottages that made up their village and then ran off deep into the scattered olive groves, cork trees and pines.

Standing at its centre was a tall, thick pole, around which bundles of firewood had been piled. Dry sticks that broke at the touch, tinder that would burn furiously within seconds of being lit.

They took her body off the boat, lifting it and tying it to the back of the donkey, the donkey that had once belonged to the priest but which was now of little use to him. Slowly, the animal moved across the ground, away from the beach and along the red dust of the road, led by a small group of men. Dogs ran at their heels, barking, sniffing and jumping up at whatever it was the donkey was carrying, yelping whenever a well-aimed stone told them to keep away.

In the distance, the men could now see the tall, dark outline of the pyre. The people standing round it. Shepherds from the countryside, men rarely seen from one market to the next. The farmers who scratched a meagre living from the hard, unfriendly soil. The fruit-growers who prayed that the weather would be kind to the handfuls of olives that trailed from the branches of their trees. The women dressed in long, billowing black dresses. The children in rags. The monk who had once loved her.

They reached the pyre. Making a soft, clicking sound out of the side of his mouth, one of the men brought the donkey to a halt. He wiped his face with the dirty, pale blue handkerchief he wore knotted round his neck. Above, the hot sun of midday glared at the dusty earth from a deep blue sky.

Slowly, the men lifted the body from the back of the donkey. A rope was thrown across the pyre. One end was tied to her throat. At the other, four men from the village now began to pull, and slowly, the body was drawn up and on to the fire, the kindling wood crackling and snapping as it bore the weight.

And still no one spoke. Some had turned away. Others stared at the ground. A child had taken a stone and was now throwing it into the scrub for one of the dogs to chase.

The body was still, lying across the top of the pyre, held in place by the rope which had been wound round the centre pole.

Three men who had been holding the torches now stepped forward. The smoke from them drifted upwards into the sky. They glanced at each other. One nodded. Without looking up, they thrust the burning swatches of grass into the base of the pyre and then moved back quickly as the flames began to search greedily through the dry timber. Within moments, thick, bright flames were coursing through the stack, reaching up, grasping for the next level.

What had been a simple pile of wood had suddenly become a pillar of flame, burning with an intensity that seemed to dim the very light of the sun. Higher and higher the flames reached, blinding those who looked too closely, entirely shrouding any sight of the firewood or of the woman's body.

And from the flames grew the smoke. The thin blue smoke that would spiral straight up into the evening skies to tell of the death of the lobisomen. Or blow to the right or to the left to make a promise of her return.

*   *   *

The fire burnt through the night and, as the first grey streaks of dawn appeared in the skies, so the men were now to be found digging a hole at its side. A deep hole into which they would shovel the ashes from the fire. The hole would then be filled in and a white, stone pillar erected over it. For so it always was across the Algarve. Whenever the lobisomen appeared.

And, as the sun began to rise into the sky, so the sequoia were seen. Floating in ever-widening circles as they drifted across the deepening blue sky. Broad-winged, each wing white but edged in black. Tragedy fused with the innocence of a life long stolen.

The sequoia. The souls of the victims of the lobisomen. Calling quietly to each other, high above the grave.

Many nights later, when the moon moved slowly behind the banks of cloud that drifted across the skies of the Algarve night, the monk, who had once loved her, dug deep beneath the pillar.

He worked quickly, cutting at the ground with a small spade, rounding the hole with his hands, scratching at the earth that grew moist as he burrowed into it. Until, finally, his hands touched the soft dust that was the remains of the fire and of the body it had burnt.

He pushed his hands into the dust, taking it in his fists, drawing it from the hole and putting it into

9

two small metal urns that he had carried to the grave. And, when both were filled, he stood up, pulling over his head the long, greasy monk's robes that he wore, and throwing them into the hole beneath the pillar.

Then he knelt and packed the loose earth over them, filling the hole and burying what was left of his past.

And finally, when he had finished, he turned away from the pillar, wearing the threadbare clothes of a peasant farmer and holding the two urns in his hands. One he would send to her father. The other, he would keep hidden on the plains of the Algarve.

1

The tall eucalyptus trees stood at the centre of the wetlands, pointing to the sky like the gaunt fingers of giants, slowly drowning in the marshes.

Here, the spiders and the lizards of the Algarve crawled without fear of man. Terrapins floated in the ink-black rivulets that threaded their way through the damp, rotting weeds. Long, thin green snakes curled into the muddy depths of stagnant pools. Or crawled through the skulls of those who had drowned there, their bodies long since dismembered and their bones now whitening in the sun.

Above the trees, a large solitary bird flew slowly round in wide circles, as if looking for its home. Long legs trailed behind it. Its head was thrust forward, its broad wings moving gently through the air.

"What is it?"

Denny stood at the edge of the wetlands, her hand above her eyes, shielding her gaze from the glare of the mid-morning sun.

"They're a kind of heron," said Elliott, watching as the bird began to move down through the sky towards the trees. "The locals call them 'the sequoia'."

"The what?"

"The sequoia. Which is a bit confusing, I suppose, since it's also the name of a giant Californian pine-tree."

Denny laughed, imagining, for a moment, flocks of giant pine-trees drifting through the summer skies of Portugal. And Elliott looked across at her, smiling. It was the first time he'd heard Denny laugh since she'd arrived.

A dusty track ran alongside the marshes, worn into the ground by the centuries of fishermen walking down to the beaches beyond. As they wandered slowly along it, Denny thought of asking her uncle about Isobel. The woman he'd married soon after leaving England to settle in the Algarve.

She thought of asking. But she didn't.

Shortly after they had moved into the villa, Isobel had been driving home, after shopping in Vilfeira, when her small sports car had left the cliffs and buried itself in the cold, rolling waters of the Atlantic.

Denny was reluctant to raise the ghost.

She looked across to the eucalyptus trees. Large bundles of sticks seemed to perch precariously on the thin, tapering branches. She stopped.

"Are those nests?"

Elliott nodded.

"They're held in place with dried mud."

"Plenty of it around," said Denny.

One by one, a flock of the sequoia began to leave the trees. Spreading their wings, pushing them through the air, moving away from the eucalyptus.

They flew low over the marshes, almost as if looking for something. Or someone. They made no noise. Even as they approached her, Denny heard nothing. No call. No soft beat of the wings as they flew overhead and then turned, floating away over the wetlands once more.

"The victims' souls," said Elliott.

Denny turned.

"Victims?"

"Of the lobisomen."

They began to walk again, the mid-morning sun now warm on their backs.

Despite the heat, the monk still wore a thick cowl over his head as he walked among the ruins that surrounded him.

The monastery had once risen majestically from the hills that sloped down towards the dusty plains of Vilfeira below.

It was said that it had taken over a hundred years to build. That huge stone pillars, each one the width of a road, had once supported the wide, vaulted, extravagantly carved ceilings. That the floors had been made up of broad, sparkling blue stones, quarried in the country's northern hills. And that the light from the thousands of candles that had filled it could be seen from the furthest horizon of the open seas it faced – an inspiration for those sailing to the New World and a welcome home for those who had found it.

And, at its centre, the five golden crosses of Santa Venezia, each one fashioned from the white gold once buried deep in the mountains of Africa. Each one taller than the pilgrims that knelt before it. Each one worth more than their lives.

But that had been before the earthquakes.

Before the first morning of November in 1755 when three massive tremors had hit Portugal, killing over sixty thousand people and levelling almost every major building in the land.

The monastery had simply collapsed, burying the monks and pilgrims inside it under thousands of tons of stone, much of which had then plunged down the side of the hill, a landslide scarring the ground and destroying the small cottages, cattle and people in its path.

All that now remained of the monastery of Santa Venezia da Vilfeira were the broken, overgrown foundation stones and a small chapel which, because it had been built into the rock of the hill itself, had miraculously survived the chaos of what had been All Saints' Day. The Day of the Dead.

It had long since fallen into disrepair, despite the efforts of the succession of solitary hermits who lived there in the years that followed. Much of the plaster that had once covered the thick stone walls had fallen to the ground. Tangled, thick weaves of ivy clutched at its framework, as if to pull the small building to the ground. The thick, once proud wooden doors that filled the marble-pillared doorway were now split, faded, rotten.

But the man who now opened them, letting the bright sunlight of the morning spill into the small chapel, had no thought for their repair.

For over two hundred years, the lonely hermits of the Cappella dos Ossos had waited. And now, at last, the monk knew that the moment was at hand.

The sequoia were gathering in a corner of the wetlands. As the minutes had passed, so more and more of them had left the eucalyptus trees, circling round the marshes until finally joining the flock.

"They'll start climbing in a moment," said

Elliott. "In a few minutes, they'll be no more than dots in the sky. And then they'll drift. Gliding on the warm air currents coming off the land."

Elliott and Denny now stood at the edges of the beach, looking back towards the birds. Behind them, they could hear the waves of the Atlantic breaking softly on the shoreline. And smell the salt in the air.

"What's the lobisomen?" said Denny.

Elliott watched the birds.

"An old story, that's all. Something to frighten the kids with at bedtime."

"It's odd, isn't it?" said Denny, turning to look out across the shingle of the short beach and the open sea beyond. "I've always wondered why anyone should ever want to scare children at bedtime."

"To let them know what will happen if they don't go to sleep," said Elliott, smiling.

"And what *would* happen?" Denny looked at him. "Who is the lobisomen?"

It was cold inside the chapel.

Pausing for a moment, letting his eyes adjust to the shadows after the glare of the sun outside, the monk stood quite still. The soft splashing of water echoed from the walls as it bubbled into the small, circular well cut into the floor at the centre of the room.

The monk spent many hours here. Listening to the sound of the water. Watching as the ripples spread across its dark surface. Sheltered from the chaos of the world beyond the wooden doors. And yet, he knew that he must now talk to that world.

He moved forwards, stepping quietly across the marble of the floor. The rope was at the far side of the chapel. Hanging limp, stretching to the ceiling, reaching through the small cut in the roof, above which hung the bell.

The sound of the bell would bring them. Perhaps in an hour. Perhaps more. Life was slow on the Algarve. And for those whose bones now hung from the walls of the chapel, so also had been their death.

They stood at the edge of the sea.

Here, the beach was deserted. There was little sand. Little for the holiday-maker. Even the sea-floor dipped sharply just beyond the water-line, making it dangerous for the less experienced swimmer. And, when the winds blew offshore, they blew the thick, sweet smell of the wetlands across the dusty shingle.

"Lobisomen. . . I suppose, literally, the word means woman-wolf."

"What? Like a female wolf?"

"No," said Elliott, watching as a small gull splashed down into the waves. "More like a werewolf. Or a vampire."

"And things that go bump in the night?" smiled Denny.

"Something like that," said Elliott, as the gull rose out of the water again, a small, wriggling fish in its beak. "The lobisomen was supposed to have been the spirit of a witch killed on the plains hundreds of years ago. Not that they did much of a job because she came back again."

"As a ghost?"

"Not quite. She had a nasty habit of killing people and then taking over their bodies. In fact," Elliott picked up a small pebble and flicked it thoughtfully towards the sea, "I seem to remember reading that there's some kind of worm that does that. But I can't remember what it's called."

Denny smiled.

"Maybe it's the lobisomen worm."

Elliott threw another pebble, this time trying to skim it across the shifting patterns of the waves.

"The legend says she was betrayed by her sister, so she always attacked women. All the women in a family, so the family would never have children again. Then she moved on to the next one."

"Charming."

Denny watched Elliott as he skimmed another pebble across the water. It bounced three times before sinking into the waves.

"It almost sounds as if you believe it."

Elliott laughed.

"I don't. Any more than I believe that those are the souls of her victims."

Denny followed the turn of his head, looking high into the sky above the wetlands.

"The sequoia?"

"Apparently," said Elliott. "Condemned never to see Paradise until the lobisomen herself is finally killed."

Denny looked at him.

"You mean she's still around?"

"Well, if she is, it's not for any lack of effort on the monks' part."

"What monks?"

"There was a monastery once." Elliott nodded towards the inland hills that ran along the skyline. "Up there. Some peculiar sect that thought they'd sorted out what life was all about. And death, I suppose. Over the years, they killed hundreds of women. And girls. Just trying to find which ones were possessed by the lobisomen."

"And if they found one?"

"They gave them to the locals to burn. They say the last one was some young fishing-girl."

"So no more lobisomen?"

Elliott smiled.

"Like all good stories, the rumour is that she'll come back again one day." He waved towards the eucalyptus trees. "And, of course, the birds are still here, so, clearly, she can't be dead."

He started walking again.

"But you'll be pleased to hear that the fishing-girl got her revenge on the monks because two years later, their monastery collapsed, killing the lot of them."

Denny smiled and then turned back towards the birds, the victims' souls. She remembered them as they had passed her. That they had seemed to be looking for something. Someone perhaps.

"Now I know why they looked so sad."

And she watched them, drifting on the air currents high above. Small, angled shapes, motionless in their flight.

The monk watched them as they moved up the hill. Walking in single file, one after another, lifting their heads occasionally to look at the chapel above them, otherwise watching the ground. They moved slowly. It was hot. And they were afraid.

There were twelve. The monk frowned. There should have been thirteen. Then, lower down the slopes of the hill, he saw the last man. Hurrying to catch the others, scrabbling awkwardly across the crumbling shale of the hillside.

Once, many years before, they had tried to carry the cage with only twelve. At the last moment, one of the men, the *mordomos*, had twisted his ankle, forcing him to hobble painfully home. For much of the procession, he had not been missed.

Until the last street. The Rua da Galacia.

There, in the centre of the town, the tall, crimson flames of the funeral pyre reaching into the deep night skies above them, one of the *mordomos* had stumbled. The cage was suddenly unbalanced, its weight moving from one side to the other, as the man fell, losing his grip. Where thirteen might have been enough to carry the cage, twelve, and now eleven, could not. It must fall. Desperately, they had tried to recover control, grabbing at the wooden cradle, trying to soak up its yawing, see-saw motion with the muscles of their arms.

The crowds at either side of the street had backed away, staring in horror as the strength of the men had suddenly seemed to give way. Two of them on the right-hand side collapsed. The cage now lurched to that side, crashing against the side of the cradle, splintering the wood and finally toppling on to the street where the wooden bars shattered on the cold, stone cobbles.

For many years afterwards, it was said that the blood of the four men crushed beneath it was to be seen running between the stones on the eve of each year's procession. The number thirteen kept the Devil at bay. The number eleven could not. Such was the lore of the countryside of the Algarve.

The monk watched the men as they now approached, some clearly tired by the climb up the steep slope. They wore the simple clothes of the Algarvean countryside. The unbuttoned, black waistcoat. The scuffed boots. The lopsided hat. The brightly coloured scarf and loose-necked shirt. Two were old. Another limped. The one who had been late, the thirteenth, had a deep red scar across the back of his hand.

They had walked without talking and still remained silent as they stood, finally, before the monk.

After some moments, he raised a hand.

"Thank you for coming. *Obrigado*."

No one replied. They knew why they had come. But not what they would see.

"We should go in now."

The monk's voice was quiet, almost as if in reverence.

He turned and walked through the half-opened doors into the chapel. After a moment's hesitation, the older man followed, beckoning to the others.

No more than a few hours ago they had been at work in the fields and orchards that lay scattered across the plains behind Vilfeira. Then they had heard the bell. Had run to their homes, shouting goodbye to anyone who might have heard them. And then climbed the hill.

And now they stood, forming a circle around the well in the Cappella dos Ossos, looking down at the water, listening to the soft splashing of the small stream that fed it.

Without speaking, the monk now held his hand over the well. He opened his fingers, dropping a small stone into the water. It splashed and then was gone, dropping through the unseen depths below. The ripples formed, spreading slowly in widening circles towards the edges where they met the stone wall and turned back upon themselves.

And through the broken surface, through the movement of the circles and at their centre, there now appeared the face of a woman. Proud. Strong. Her cheekbones high. The trace of a smile on her lips. Dark hair that framed the silhouette of a thin, angular, white face.

And deep, dark holes where her eyes had once been.

2

The jeep bounced crazily as it sped along the dusty, pot-holed track. Once, there had been an attempt to lay tarmac on its surface. But it had long since crumbled, the remaining black swathes now cracked and no more than scars on the surface of the hard, rutted earth.

Elliott shifted his foot, leaving the accelerator and now jamming on the brake pedal. The jeep slowed, stopping finally at the side of the road.

"What is it?" said Denny, wiping her hand across her face, pushing the hair out of her eyes. Behind them a swirl of dust still hung in the warm, heavy air of the afternoon, thrown up by broad tyres of the jeep.

"I thought you might want to see it," said Elliott.

At the opposite side of the road, a worn, weatherbeaten stone seemed to grow out of the dusty Portuguese ground. It leant over at an angle. Almost as if pulled there. Or pushed from beneath.

Its sides were straight.

Denny jumped out of the jeep and walked slowly across towards it.

Elliott followed her.

"It's where they buried her."

"Who?" said Denny.

"The last one they burnt. The fishing girl."

Denny looked up.

"It's horrible."

Elliott shook his head.

"They were simple people."

Denny turned back to look at the stone.

"Then God save us from simple people."

In the distance, across the dry, parched fields, a bell rang. A small bell. Hanging from the neck of a goat, as it grazed among the shrivelled bushes. And beyond the goat stood a figure, unmoving, poorly clothed, almost shimmering in the heat, as if no more than a mirage among the dried grasses.

"But it gives them a good excuse for a party," said Elliott, turning back towards the jeep.

"Party?"

Denny was still standing by the stone, her hand touching its worn, pitted surface.

"Every summer. In fact, next week. If you want to—"

"What do they do?"

"The usual kind of Portuguese thing," said Elliott. "Everyone gets dressed up, they make a lot of noise, there's a big procession and then a bonfire."

"And what's it got to do with her?" said Denny, looking down again at the stone beside her.

"She's the reason for the bonfire," said Elliott, climbing back into the jeep. "They put a life-size dummy of her in a wooden cage, carry it through the town and then throw it on the fire."

"Like Guy Fawkes night?"

"Absolutely. It's their way of making sure that the lobisomen doesn't come back."

The goat's bell was closer now. Denny glanced up, looking for the animal.

"Who's that with the goat?"

Elliott turned his head towards the distant figure, still seemingly motionless in the glare of the sun.

"They call him the shepherd. *O Pastor*. He seems to spend his life walking across the plains with his animals. Mad as a hatter but quite harmless."

He flicked the key and the jeep's engine growled into life.

"You coming?"

Denny turned.

"Do you mind if I walk? I mean, I don't think it's very far and I just. . ."

"It's fine," said Elliott. He knew she needed the space. Time to herself. It would take her a long time to get over what had happened to her friend. "Straight up the road, turn left at the top. It's about a mile from there."

He turned the wheel and began to move away.

"I thought we'd eat about seven. That OK?"

"I'll be there." said Denny, waving as the jeep picked up speed. Some moments later, it had gone, the noise of its engine tailing away as the peace of the late afternoon once more fell on the flat, dry wasteland.

She found herself studying the stone pillar again. There seemed to be an inscription, chiselled into the dull, grey stone. Denny leant down, looking more closely.

She couldn't read it. Over the passing years, the winds had whipped their sand and grit across the countryside and worn away the sharpened edges of the letters. There might have been two words. Perhaps it had been the woman's name.

She put out her hand, tracing the letters with her finger.

The first word was "In". The second was longer, starting with an "S", closing with an "s". Denny worked her finger across the uneven surface for some minutes. Conjuring up words that might have made sense. But didn't. Seagrass. Sunless. Spotless.

The bell startled her.

She straightened, twisting quickly towards the noise. And found herself being watched by the goat. The animal stood quite still, its dark eyes watching Denny carefully, the rusty bell on the rope around its neck swinging slowly from side to side. It seemed old. Its coat was worn, the hair grey at the sides of its mouth.

Denny took a step forwards. Still the goat did not move. She reached out a hand, whispering quietly to the creature, as if talking to a baby. Somehow, she knew it wouldn't hurt her. She bent down and moved her hand towards its forehead. She stroked it. Felt the coarse, wiry hair run through her fingers. Let her hand run down the stiff, broad bone of its nose. Looked into its eyes, each dark circle split in half by the yellow slash of its pupil.

And then she stood, smiling.

"You look hot."

The goat bowed its head, turned and moved some yards away, where it began to pick with its teeth at a small, tinder-dry bush. There had been a look in its eyes. One of sadness, perhaps.

She turned again to the pillar, studying the worn inscription. And then, quite suddenly, it was clear. Just as the image emerges from a brass-rubbing or a small boat from the fog, so the words chiselled into the stone, so long ago, once more came to life.

In Spiritus.

She stood back quickly, her pulse quickening, the

memory of the words on the cathedral gravestone suddenly rearing at the edges of her mind.

"They won't hurt, you know. They're only words."

Denny twisted round, startled by the voice.

"Who—?"

The shepherd was standing some yards away, close to the goat. A tall stick in his right hand, his left holding a small, clay pipe that he would put to his mouth from time to time. He spoke softly.

"Just a shepherd," he said. "No name. Haven't had a name for years. You don't need a name just to wander round the plains."

He took the pipe out of his mouth and pointed towards the pillar.

"Just words. No harm in them."

"It's just . . . just that I've seen them before," said Denny.

The shepherd nodded slowly.

"I know. I told him to put them there. On the gravestone. I told him in the letter. But they're only words."

"Letter?"

Denny remembered what Elliott had said. She was glad he'd used the word "harmless".

"I wrote him a letter. I had to explain what had happened. Seemed only fair." He lifted his pipe again, sucking gently at it, letting the smoke drift from the corners of his mouth. "But it's all so long ago now."

And then, as if, suddenly, the memory of whatever letter it had been had brought the conversation to an end, he began to turn away, gently clicking his tongue, encouraging the goat to follow him.

"Just a minute. . ." Denny raised her voice, calling to him. "You're speaking English. Are you English?"

The man turned, smiling briefly.

"I was. Once upon a time."

And, with a last smile, he turned away again and soon his gaunt figure was melting into the dried, jumbled landscape. He had wondered what she would look like.

Denny watched him go. And then turned and began to walk. As mad as a hatter, just as Elliott had said.

Overhead, the sun had begun to drop towards the west. And yet the heat remained. And would do so long into the evening and through the night. As she walked, Denny could feel the sweat seeping through her skin and running across her face.

She glanced up the road. Earlier, she thought she had seen something. Someone perhaps. A trace. A shadow. A mirage.

But there had been no one. Only the road. At either side, the stunted cork trees. The thin, wispy branches of the light green pines. The dried balls of grass that drifted across the dust and the stones.

Elliott would be wondering where she was. He might even come back to look for her. Denny smiled to herself. After half an hour of walking through the Algarvean heat, the sight of his jeep would be a welcome one.

She looked up.

This time, there was someone. Denny could see her quite clearly. The woman was standing by the side of the road. Tall. A black shawl draped across her bowed head. The black clothes of the Portuguese countryside falling from her shoulders and about her body.

Her head was shaded but, as Denny walked, she knew the woman was watching her. Waiting for her.

At the sight of the goat, Denny had been startled. The sight of the woman prompted a quite different feeling. As she drew closer to her, Denny was almost surprised to find it was fear.

It was just a woman. A mother. A farmer's wife. Walking her dog on her way home from the village market, her basket filled with fruit. With bread. And with fresh fish bought from the softly-spoken fishermen on the beaches.

But there was no dog. No basket. No fish.

"Boa tard," said Denny, as she slowly passed the woman. Her voice was quiet, hoarse. The words meant "good afternoon" but their warmth was not returned.

The woman did not look up.

Denny hesitated, wondering whether to say more. And then the woman spoke. So softly that Denny barely heard her. She bent forwards, closing out the sounds of the afternoon, trying to pick out the words.

And then she understood.

She straightened quickly, turning, now running, pushing herself up the hill, suddenly desperate to reach its top, the turning left, the sight of Vilfeira. The sight of people. She ran, almost expecting to hear footsteps behind, following her, chasing her. To feel hands clutching at her clothes and her body. To hear the woman screaming, shrieking.

She reached the corner and slowed. Her breathing hard, taut, almost painful. Her heart and pulse pumping hard as her blood coursed through them.

She turned quickly, staring back down the track. The woman was still there. Her head lifted now but her face too distant to be seen.

The woman who stood by the side of a dusty track and had whispered the words, "In Spiritus".

And as Denny watched, high above, a large white bird spread its wings and drifted on the warm currents of air that rose from the plains of the Algarve.

By seven, the sun was beginning to set.

Looking out across Bahia Azur, the "blue bay", they sat on the stone patio, watching the reddening skies of the west and the long shadows now being thrown across the ground by the tall pines that surrounded the villa. The waters of the bay were quiet, the breeze of the afternoon having eased, the only movement being the gentle swell that ran in from the Atlantic Ocean beyond.

Elliott raised his glass to his mouth, sipping the red wine slowly. On such an evening, as the background colours of the sky threw the horizon into the silhouette of a thin, razored line running across the skies, Elliott could understand why the seas of Portugal were once thought to run along the edges of the world.

He put his glass back on the table.

"Maybe she was saying something completely different. Something in Portuguese."

"Maybe," said Denny, quietly. "But I don't think so."

Across the bay, in the shadows of the headland that towered over them, the lights of the distant town of Vilfeira were beginning to sparkle.

Elliott turned in his chair, looking at his niece. It had been his suggestion that she should come out to Portugal. After what had happened, she needed to get away. There would be no one in Portugal that she knew. No faces to bring back the memories. No memories, apart from those she would carry in her head. And those, she would carry for the rest of her life. In Portugal, she might be able to relax.

But the bizarre story of the woman frightened him. The death of her friend had clearly affected Denny very much more seriously than Elliott had at first imagined.

"Would it help if you talked about Leyla?"

Denny shook her head slowly.

"I don't think I can. Not yet, anyway." She looked across the table towards her uncle. "But that was kind of you."

Elliott smiled.

"You will get over it, you know. It just takes time."

Denny, nodded, standing up from the chair, turning her head once again towards the colours of the evening sky.

"I know."

3

The wind was blowing from the east. The "Levanter" east. It wasn't yet strong but, already, it was beginning to chase across the tops of the Atlantic waves as they rolled in towards the long golden beaches of Vilfeira.

One o'clock.

During the afternoon, the wind would strengthen. Only to die away by the evening. That was the weather pattern of the Algarvean coast, during the long dog days of the summer.

As she watched the holiday-makers on the beaches below Jamie's Bar, Denny wondered how many of them knew. Maybe her uncle was right. Maybe they should have put up a notice to remind the unwary that the winds could change very suddenly and very quickly. That they overturned fishing boats and that they drowned small children, playing in each wave, shrieking with laughter, unaware that the next one could kill them.

She was drinking orange juice.

Jamie's Bar opened for the summer months. During the winter the visitors played golf. Or went inland to seek out the monuments, the castles and the ruins, scattered across the mountains of the north or the wide, flat Alentejo plains of the south. They didn't go to the beach.

"You would like another one, senora?"

Jamie was standing beside her. Denny drank what was left in her glass and glanced up at him.

"I thought I might have something to eat."

"Sure. We got sardines. You like sardines? Or maybe some squid?"

Denny smiled. When he'd dropped her at the bar and introduced her to Jamie, Elliott had told her that sardines and squid were all Jamie's Bar ever had to eat. "Sardines would be good."

"And some bread?"

"And another orange juice."

Denny smiled again and added the Portuguese for "thank you". "*Obrigada*."

Jamie grinned. Denny's pronunciation was hopeless but at least she'd tried. Most of them didn't bother.

"I ask Joaquim to get it for you." He nodded towards a waiter, busy setting another table. "You on holiday?"

Denny nodded.

"Sort of."

"You have good time, then."

He smiled and began to walk away. Denny watched him go.

"Sure."

She let her gaze drift over the small cabin and the surrounding assortment of tables and parasols that was Jamie's Bar. Some of the tables sat on uneven wooden planking that ran round the building. Others were simply stuck in the sand. All were turned to face the beaches below and the wide expanse of sea beyond.

It wasn't busy.

A young couple sat at one table nearby, their heads close together, their conversation bright, their laughter spontaneous. A family of four sat in silence, picking at platefuls of Jamie's sardines. A rather serious-looking young man sat at the bar, smoking a cigarette and drinking a chilled beer.

A group of children appeared, taking a short cut through the tables of the bar, on their way to the beach. They were followed by a tall, greying man with a vivid yellow shirt. He looked bored.

Maybe he doesn't like beaches, thought Denny. Or even kids.

One of the boys in the group had a ball which he was throwing to another, as they made their way across the sand and through the jumble of Jamie's tables.

The ball flew high into the air. Bright, colourful, sparkling against the deep blue sky above. It had been thrown too hard. Spinning, it reached the top of its climb and then slowly drifted back down towards the sand.

As it did so, for the first time, Denny noticed the woman who was standing just beyond the last tables of Jamie's Bar. She wore dark glasses and a wide, dirty, straw hat pulled down over her face against the bright glare of the sun.

The ball landed beside her. She didn't move. Neither to scold the child nor to help him retrieve the ball. The boy walked forwards, slowly. From a distance, he seemed to have said something to her. The woman didn't respond.

Beside her, the boy looked small.

The waiter appeared, a broad smile on his face, a basket of bread rolls in one hand, cutlery in the other.

"I hope you're hungry."

He stood beside Denny, blocking her view of the woman.

"I . . . er. . ."

Denny faltered, suddenly realizing that she was alone in a Portuguese bar and didn't speak Portuguese.

"Don't worry." The waiter smiled. "I speak English. Well, some English, anyway."

He began to clear the table, sweeping the sand off its surface with his hands, putting the rolls down, picking up Denny's glass. She watched him, smiling, "What's your name?"

The waiter stopped.

"Me? Joaquim. And you?

"Denny."

"It's a nice name."

"So's Joaquim."

Joaquim laughed. "Then we must both be very nice people. Another juice?"

Denny smiled, nodding.

"Yes, please."

And Joaquim turned and was gone. At that moment, Denny realized who the woman was. The woman who was sitting two tables away. Staring at her.

Already, the banners were going up. Stretched across the small squares and alleyways, hanging from open windows or trailing from the labyrinth of telephone wires that criss-crossed the town's main streets, their brilliant colours brought a sense of festival to Vilfeira.

Fogo de Artefício. The festival of the Fire.

It was cooler in the bank, even if the air-conditioning wasn't working perfectly. A small, handwritten notice explained that one of the motors had failed but that the manager was arranging for it to be replaced. Very soon. The last two words were underlined.

There was only one queue.

A man and a woman stood at its head, arguing with the cashier. Elliott couldn't pick up their accent. It might have been German. Or Scandinavian. The argument seemed to be about the exchange rate. And it had been going on for just over fifteen minutes.

Elliott glanced up at the large, metal clock hanging on the wall behind the cashier. Nearly one o'clock. He'd left Denny at midday. Maybe she would have had something to eat.

She couldn't turn the tap.

Her hand was shaking so violently that she seemed to have lost all control of it. With her other hand, Denny gripped the small, metal basin, knowing that if she let go, she would fall to the floor. Her legs were weak. Almost without any feeling. Every so often she would glance fearfully, quickly, over her shoulder, half-expecting the woman to be there. The white face. The glasses. The black shawl slung over her shoulders.

But the small room was empty. Dark on a day of sunshine, the only light filtering in through the small air vents, cut high into the wooden walls.

*   *   *

The sardines smelt good.

Joaquim whistled softly to himself as he pushed them backwards and forwards with a knife across the thin, metal bars of the grill. The charcoal glowed beneath them, bursting every so often into flame as oil dripped from the burning fish.

The barbecue stood to one side of the bar and as Joaquim worked, he let his gaze wander absent-mindedly over the tables outside. The girl had brushed past him, quickly, mumbling an apology. She had to go to the washroom. She'd be back in a minute. He'd heard the door slam.

Now another woman came into the bar, her head bowed, her features hidden beneath a broad hat. She looked vaguely familiar but against the sunshine outside, she was little more than a silhouette, a shadow. Without speaking, she crossed the floor, passed Joaquim and disappeared into the short corridor that led to the washroom.

"It's busy!" shouted Joaquim.

He shrugged his shoulders as Jamie glanced across from the far side of the bar, where he was pouring a glass of cold beer.

"She'll find out soon enough," said Joaquim, almost to himself as he turned back to the sardines, flipping them over with the knife.

They both heard the scream.

Dropping the glass, letting it shatter on the polished tiles of the floor, Jamie threw himself across the room. A second scream. A scream of fear. Of panic. Joaquim clenched the knife in his fist, almost falling over Jamie as they crashed into the corridor, bouncing off the walls, desperate to throw open the washroom door, terrified of what they might see.

Jamie kicked at the door, so viciously that it broke from its hinges near the floor, crashing lop-sidedly into the wall. The crash echoed round the small room.

"What—?"

The girl was on the floor, screaming, shaking. The floor around her wet, the basin overflowing. Jamie ran to her, kneeling down, taking her head in his hands, wiping her face with a shirtsleeve.

"But, I saw. . ." said Joaquim, standing quite still, the knife still in his hand.

He stepped back into the corridor. Nothing. Only the smell of burning fish, drifting from the bar.

The water was cold.

The surface had been warm, heated by the glare of the sun throughout the day. But along the bottom of the pool, where Denny now swam, the water would always run cold.

Her eyes were open. Staring ahead through the filtered, clear water. Slowly, she let the sweep of her arms pull her forwards, her shadow moving across the intricate blue-and-white patterns of the tiles beneath her.

The *azulejos*.

The famous tiles of Portugal that had decorated the altars and church walls of the country for a thousand years, now reduced to paving the bottom of a swimming-pool.

Denny smiled and then began to move upwards through the water, her legs kicking her up towards the shadows of the late afternoon that stretched across the pool.

As she broke the surface she saw Elliott standing by the poolside table. At first he said nothing, simply lifting a cup of coffee to his mouth. Slowly Denny swam to the side of the pool, pulling herself out, picking up her towel from one of the wooden garden chairs.

"Feeling any better?"

"Fine," said Denny, sitting in the chair, leaning back, letting the sunlight warm her.

"I think Jamie must be right."

Elliott remained standing, gazing across the villa's lawn towards the pines and olive trees that bordered the garden.

"It must have been some kind of mugger."

Denny said nothing.

"I mean, it's even possible that you're right. Maybe it is the same woman that you saw the other day.

"Yesterday," said Denny, her eyes closed.

"OK, yesterday."

"And it was the same woman. Only yesterday, I. . ."

Denny was sitting up now, the memory of Jamie's bar suddenly vivid once again. The quiet opening of the door. The shadow that joined her in the room. The whispered words. The hand that lifted the glasses away from the white, porcelain face.

Suddenly she stood, her body shaking, the sweat breaking on her forehead. Elliott moved quickly to her, grabbed her, held her as the tears once more began to slide down her face.

He found it difficult to imagine what Denny had said she had seen. Difficult to imagine the woman's face. Smiling. But with no eyes.

4

Denny woke.
For some moments, she lay quite still, letting the nightmare pass. Letting the images slowly disappear, melting into the dark corners of the bedroom.

She turned her head, glancing towards the small clock at her bedside. Its luminous numbers glowed clearly in the dark, Quarter past two.

It was warm.

Through the open window, Denny thought she could hear an owl calling amongst the pines. Perhaps in answer to the endless chatter of the cicadas that seemed to surround the small, whitewashed villa.

She swung her legs out of the bed, pulling the

thin white sheet over her shoulders. Slowly she walked across the floor, almost grateful for the touch of the cold stone tiles on the soles of her feet. The bedroom door was open. She walked through and out on to the veranda, the soft scents of the flowers of the Algarve drifting across the shadows.

She stood, looking out into the night. Wrapped in white, a pale ghost, alone in the starlight.

She didn't notice the movement at first.

And, when she did, she thought of her dream. And then of the gardener. What was he called? Emilio? Then she remembered the small, glowing clock-face. Quarter past two. It wasn't Emilio.

Perhaps it wasn't anyone at all. Just the wind touching the withered carob pods or sifting through the thick, massed leaves of the stubby orange trees.

And then she saw the outline of the figure. Caught in the half-light left by the stars across the open ground. Tall. Walking quickly, almost shapeless, the contours and movement of the body disguised by the long sweep of a cloak.

The figure had been crossing from right to left, moving from a group of tall spindly pines towards the deep shadows of the olive trees. When, suddenly, it had stopped – as if seeing Denny for the first time. Held in the dim light, it had remained motionless for some moments and then turning, it started towards the villa, moving more quickly now. And without a noise.

Denny stood, staring. Almost as if hypnotized.

Then, suddenly, she turned, running inside the villa, slamming the door behind her. Hammering the bolt home.

She ran into her bedroom, throwing herself across the floor, grabbing the tall shutters at either side of the window.

Glancing briefly through its glass, she caught sight of the figure, moving quickly across the dark, flat lawn that ran up to the doors of the house.

Denny swung both shutters together, startled by the splintering crash of wood as they met. She reached for the iron bar that would pin them together. It jammed. She pushed against the shutters, her right hand punching the bar, her knuckles bleeding.

And then, suddenly, it shifted, sliding through the handles of the shutters, locking them together.

Denny let herself slip to the floor, where she sat on the cold tiles, her shoulders heaving as her lungs searched for air. And yet she tried to still the movement. To hold her body stiff, her breathing silent, as she listened.

There was nothing. No sound. Apart from the cicadas, their chorus muted by the closed, wooden shutters. She glanced across at the clock. Half past two. She listened. Nothing.

And then the scratching. Faint at first, but then growing louder, more intent, as someone outside now began to claw at the shutters. Fingernails stripping the wood. And then fists that hammered against it.

The shutters slammed inwards, the iron of their hinges squealing under the impact, the wood cracking, the iron bar clattering against the thick wooden slats.

Denny began to scream.

The bedroom door was suddenly open.

"Denny!"

And then the silence returned. Suddenly. Like the final drop of a guillotine blade.

Elliott was standing in the doorway, a torch in his hand.

"Out there!" screamed Denny. "It's out there!"

Elliott turned quickly, moving to the veranda door, breaking open the lock.

"Who's there!"

He bellowed the words, throwing the powerful beam of the torch across the gardens. But there was no one. Just the movement of the trees. And the scent of the flowers.

In the shadows, a small cat miaowed. And then moved silently back into the night.

5

As he turned his bicycle off the thin country track and into the gardens of the villa, Emilio glanced at his watch. Half past eight. He was early.

He hadn't slept well and, just after dawn, he had eased himself quietly from his bed and shuffled across the thin carpet of the bedroom floor, leaving his wife asleep, her head turned towards the crumbling plaster of the wall.

In the kitchen, he had made coffee. Black coffee. Poured himself a *medronho*, the clear spirit made from the fruit of the strawberry tree, deep in the mountains of the Serra de Monchique. Taken sparingly, it brought warmth. Taken to excess, it brought stupor and sometimes death. He had gone outside, sipping the coffee and tasting the *medronho* as the first glow of the approaching sun had begun to fill the eastern edges of the sky.

Now, as he leant the rusting bicycle against the wooden slats of the garden shed, he could still taste the *medronho*. The bittersweet tang at the back of his throat that had warmed him during the long uncomfortable ride from his small cottage. Each year he promised himself a new bicycle. And each year he broke his promise.

On Tuesdays, Emilio worked for Elliott. Every Tuesday, every week of the year. Elliott, one of the *estrangeiros*: the newcomers, who had come to live out their lives on the shores of the Algarve. Even if sometimes those lives were short.

Emilio had known Elliott's wife.

It had been Isobel who had first spoken to him. She'd seen him pruning the almond trees that shaded the roadside Café dos Dias and, pulling up in her small, green BMW, had asked him if he was free to help with her garden as well. He had been keen. Work was not always easy to find in the Algarve. Emilio had started the following week. On a Tuesday.

He'd seen the car after the crash. He remembered crying, standing amongst a small crowd on the cliffs, watching as it was dragged slowly from the waves and on to the shingle of the beach.

As he opened the door of the garden shed and

began to take out the various tools he would need during the morning, he thought of Isobel.

She had loved the garden. The brilliant colours of the spring, the soft green down of the summer and the fresh, almost tangible sense of growth brought by the rains of winter. She would stand, for hours it seemed, watching the small birds fidgeting in the branches of the pine trees. Or the swallowtail butterflies that settled on the purple blooms of the jacaranda. She'd even grown fond of the brightly coloured, tapering lizards that lived amongst the rocks, the thin leather of their skins a dazzling chequerboard of blues and yellows.

Once, Emilio had shared her love of the small creatures. Now they did no more than remind him of what had happened. And in doing so, they had become a symptom of the same evil that had killed her. The evil of the creature that had no eyes.

Isobel had been a victim of the lobisomen. But only the monk had known.

Joaquim watched his mother as she gently stirred the contents of the stained, metal pot swinging slowly backwards and forwards over the small kitchen fire.

Chicken soup. The bones of the bird they had eaten the night before, now mixed with carrots and beans. And garlic. The smell of the herb drifted across the shadows of the kitchen. Joaquim smiled.

If garlic was the cure-all that his mother held it to be, then they must surely be the healthiest family in all of southern Portugal.

"Are you working today, Joaquim?"

His mother glanced briefly across the room towards him. She seemed anxious. Joaquim nodded.

"Every day. Every week. It's summer. Maybe I get some time tomorrow."

He stood up, turning and walking to the door that opened on to the quiet, dusty road that threaded its way through the small village. Outside, his father sat on the short stone bench. Joao would be found there every morning. Leaning back against the front wall of the cottage, his arms folded, his eyes half-closed, his mind on the day ahead or on the years gone by. Sometimes he would raise a chipped, clay pipe to his mouth, blowing traces of curling, thin blue smoke into the air above him.

Earlier, he had waved to Emilio, riding past on his bicycle. Perhaps they would have a beer in the evening. Perhaps a bottle of wine at Café Julia. Perhaps.

The chill of the early morning had still been in the air as Emilio had passed by. Now, the street was warmer, the early morning sun stretching across the pan-tiled cottage roofs, a bright sun that suggested another long, hot day.

"*Bon dia, Papa.*"

Joao turned his head towards his son as he appeared at the cottage doorway.

"You'll be serving many cold beers today, Joaquim."

Joaquim smiled.

"Yes, I think so."

"That is. . ."

Joao paused, briefly.

". . . that is, if you go."

"If I go?"

"Maybe the woman. . ."

Joaquim smiled.

"A mugger. A thief. Nothing more."

Joaquim had seen her in the night. She had been in his dream. Silhouetted against the door. Moving across the room. Long, thin white fingers that had reached out towards his throat. The stains and smell of dried blood woven into the folds of the long flowing cloak that seemed to wrap about him, clutching at him, like the oily, suckered tentacles of an octopus.

And he had woken. Sweating. Breathless. Terrified. And then had known it only to have been a dream. A dream. A nightmare conjured up from the bones of stories, told long ago at his bedside. And later, when he had fallen back to sleep, the young girl had appeared. She had smiled at first and then spoken. Joaquim had not heard her voice but she seemed to be saying the same word over and over again. Almost chanting it. And then she had waved, sadness in her face, and had once more disappeared into the night.

Joaquim looked down at his father.

"Whoever the woman was, she won't be back."

"Maybe."

Joao looked away again, gazing across the rooftops of the village towards the mountains, where the climbing sun was now beginning to burn away the shadows. He had wanted to say something. To tell his son.

But he could not.

Elliott stood on the veranda, looking up at the shutters. Whatever had hit them had been powerful. Both hung limply from their upper hinges. Both were shattered, their broken wooden panels splintered, shredded by the violence of the attack.

"What was it, Emilio? What kind of creature did that?"

Emilio shook his head.

"I don't know, Señor. I have never seen. . ."

He stopped as Denny appeared at the villa doorway. At first she said nothing.

"I thought you'd like a coffee."

Elliott smiled.

"I'll do it, just. . ."

"No." Denny's voice was quiet, controlled. "No. I need to do it."

She turned and went back into the villa.

"Just take them down, Emilio." Elliott now began to pull at the shutters, jerking them, breaking off cracked spars of wood. "And then burn them."

"Señor. . ."

"I'll go into Vilfeira. I'm sure Mateus won't take too long to knock up another pair."

"Maybe an owl?"

Elliott turned, surprised.

"An owl?"

"Yes, an owl. Sometimes they grow very big."

Emilio shrugged his shoulders.

"I don't know. Maybe it lost its way. Crash into the window. Maybe."

Elliott smiled.

"Maybe."

Elliott.

Joao knew the name but not the man. Emilio worked for him.

There had been a wife. Portuguese. A lawyer from Lisbon. Joao remembered the story in the paper. She'd been shopping in the town. And then had apparently driven along the cliffs, which is where it happened. He couldn't remember her name. As he sat on the bench, watching as the stubby weathered buildings of the village slowly came to life, Joao thought it might have begun with an "I". Or maybe an "L". As the day grew older, maybe he would remember.

Standing up, he frowned briefly at the noise of the motorbike as it emerged from the thin, pot-holed track running down the side of the cottage.

"*Adios, Papa!*"

Joaquim stopped the bike for a moment at the end of the track, smiling, his thick, dark hair falling over his eyes. He brushed it back and raised his hand.

"Have a good day."

"*Adios, Joaquim.*"

Joao watched as his son twisted the machine's handlebars to the right, kicked the small metal pedal beneath the whining engine and, lifting his foot from the ground, turned on to the road and jagged across its uneven surface towards the distant outlines of Vilfeira.

"Did you say anything?"

Joao turned as his wife appeared by his shoulder. He shook his head, slowly.

"No."

"*Esta bem.*" Sofia watched their son clear the outskirts of the village. "It's all madness anyway."

By noon, the streets of Vilfeira were deserted.

Sitting in the jeep as they drove slowly through the streets, Denny thought she might have been forgiven for assuming that the entire population had been carried off by the plague.

"It's like a ghost town."

"They're all on the beaches," said Elliott. "Or in the supermarket. It's one of the only buildings in town with air-conditioning."

Briefly, he thought of the bank and its motor that would be replaced. Very soon.

The approach of the festival had meant that the town had made some effort to cheer itself up. Banners, garlands and flags now took the eye away from the dour, unwashed buildings that haunted the side streets. Shop windows, where their shutters weren't closed against the midday sun, sported bright, colourful posters that seemed to talk of music, song and dance. And, at several points along the main streets, tall, candy-striped poles had been erected, each with what seemed to be a bundle of sticks carried in a basket at the top.

"Torches," said Elliott.

"Torches?"

"For the procession. When the cage appears, they set them on fire to light the way."

Denny was silent.

"They seem to be obsessed with fire."

Elliott laughed.

"It looks terrific. And, after all, it's all supposed to be fun."

"What they did to that girl two hundred years ago wasn't very funny," said Denny, noticing a policeman who seemed to have appeared from nowhere and who was now standing on the cracked flagstones of the pavement, watching the jeep as it pulled up in front of the town's only set of traffic lights.

"But that was two hundred years ago," said Elliott, dropping into neutral, letting the jeep's engine idle as they waited for the red to change to green. "And a lot of nasty things have happened before. And since. Anyway, you'll enjoy it."

The lights changed.

"What's that?"

They were now running into the town's small square. Often it would host the local market, when housewives, farmers, fishermen, traders, thieves and tumbling, screaming children brought life and colour to the sobriety of the surrounding buildings. It had been a meeting point for the revolutionaries of 1820. And once, it had been a place of execution.

Now it stood empty, its cobblestones bathed in the glare of the sun, the small circular pond at its centre reflecting the deep, rich blue of the skies above. And at one side of the pool stood the tall pyramid of wood. Long eucalyptus stems, bundled and lashed together. Thick, gnarled branches from the cork and olive trees. Swatches of tall, thick, dried grass.

"Ah, that," said Elliott, slowing the jeep. "That's the fire."

Denny found herself staring at the towering

stack of wood. It must have taken days to prepare and yet would take no more than a few hours of one evening to destroy. And with it, the girl. A simple fishing girl. Her bones broken, her body twisted, her remains now buried deep in the dry soil of the Algarve. Despite the heat of midday, Denny felt the cold shock of fear run through her body. The same cold shock that she had known when she had first heard Leyla screaming.

"I think I could do with a beer," said Elliott, letting the jeep follow the cobbled road that led from the square to the beaches. "Jamie's place is on the way. Could you cope with that?"

It wasn't exactly on the way. But Elliott knew that to kill an unpleasant memory you had to confront it.

Denny turned, taking her gaze from the dark shadow of the fire in the square. And smiled.

"Sure. Providing I don't have to eat sardines."

The bar was busy.

Leaving the jeep at one side of the sandy track that curled through the gaunt spindly pines that seemed to stoop towards the ground, their backs bent against the cold Atlantic winds, Elliott and Denny walked down the slope of the hill towards Jamie's, hearing the sounds of the glasses and plates, catching the scent of charcoal in the air.

"You sure you're all right?"

"I'm fine," said Denny, her eyes scanning the bar,

perhaps looking for the woman. Perhaps for Joaquim. "I mean, I don't know what's been going on but. . ."

She let the sentence hang in the air, preferring to let her imagination suddenly escape into the world in front of her as they left the pines and stood above the bar.

The broad sweep of the deep blue Atlantic, moving slowly beneath the dome of the midsummer sky. The golden ribbon of sand that traced the wide semi-circle of the bay. The colours of the fishing boats that bobbed at anchor offshore or lay at crazy angles on the beach. The sounds of laughter, the screams of delight. The heady mixture of pine resin and the sharp tang of the Atlantic brine.

The Algarve. The Al-Garb of the ancient Moors. The Land to the West.

In this world, there could be no demons. No creatures that hammered at the window in the night. Or had deep black holes where their eyes should have been. In this world, no blind woman whispered, "In spiritus".

Denny caught her uncle by the arm.

"Come on. There's a table free. And it's in the shade."

Joaquim had seen them and was already waving, smiling. He was pointing to the empty table.

"Bon dia! Boa tarde! Aqui!"

"Hi!"

Denny started to run ahead and, moments later, Elliott found himself smiling to see her shaking hands with the young waiter, laughing, both of them talking at once, both so obviously pleased to see each other. He remembered how kind Denny said Joaquim had been after the woman had gone.

That was a better memory to keep.

The drinks were cold. And welcome. They drank them slowly, spinning the ice-cubes against the glass, letting the peace of the Algarvean midday wash over them. Briefly, Denny had talked of Leyla but had then quickly moved on, leaving the mention of her friend as no more than a footprint in the sand, a reminder that, one day, she would have to address her own feelings of guilt. But not now. Not in the sunshine of the Algarve.

From time to time Joaquim would join them, telling them about the family over on the right, whose young girl had earlier asked for a squid and then run out of the bar screaming when she thought she saw it move. Or the man at the bar who was drinking *medronho* under the impression that it was some kind of tonic water. The two boys who helped in the kitchen were taking bets on how long it would be before he fell over.

And for the first time in what had seemed like for ever, Denny began to relax. At the edges of an Algarvean beach, surrounded by the conversation and laughter of a small bar that served up burnt sardines and live squid and where she had found a friend in someone she knew only as Joaquim, Denny was at last able, no matter how briefly, to leave the nightmares behind.

She leant back in her chair, letting her gaze drift upwards into the sky above her, where thin traces of white cloud hung like scratches on a deep blue surface.

And where a large bird, its long, white wings spread out at either side of its body, circled slowly in the warm currents of air. The sequoia.

6

The girl came to him again in the night.

Earlier in the evening, Joaquim had sat with his father on the stone bench outside their small home, listening to the muted laughter from the Café Julia, the low growl of the occasional car moving past them, the barking of a dog, shut out of its home. He'd spoken of the day and of a girl called Denny. And of their plans for tomorrow. A ride into the hills, a picnic. A glimpse of the real Algarve.

And the older man had laughed, saying that if the girl had ever seen Joaquim drive his motorbike, she'd have stuck with the sardines in Jamie's Bar, burnt or not. And then Joao had asked if this was the same girl. The girl who they'd found screaming. Joaquim had said yes. And his father had fallen silent, the smoke from his pipe curling into the night, drifting against the bright carpet of stars high above them.

Soon afterwards, Joaquim had gone inside. He was tired. And closing the creaking wooden door to his room, he'd climbed gratefully into the thin, cotton sheets that covered the goats' hair mattress of his bed. And he'd fallen asleep, the cicadas in the almond trees no more than a distant chorus and the small lizard crawling down the side of the wall by his bed making no noise. And much later in the night, when the village slept, when no dogs barked and no cars went by, the girl had come. Drifting into his imagination. A girl with pain on her face. A girl whose lips opened but who could not be heard. Saying one word, over and over again. And who had then waved, and who had gone.

Joaquim knew where the villa was. He could remember it being built ten, maybe twelve, years before. It had been one of several put up along the edges of the beach where he and his friends had played football.

He smiled.

It could even have been from the same villa that the overweight, balding Spaniard had appeared one afternoon, shouting at them, telling them that the beach was now his and that they were trespassing. Not that they'd paid any attention. For the

Portuguese, all the Spanish were pigs and this one had been no exception. Eventually, he'd given up and gone away.

At the sound of the motorbike, Elliott glanced through the kitchen window. He turned, looking upwards.

"Denny!"

Moments later, he heard the sound of her shoes tapping down the stairway above his head.

"I hope you don't mind," she said, as she appeared in the kitchen, a canvas bag slung over her shoulder. "I took some bits and pieces from the fridge."

"I don't mind," said Elliott. "You take what you want. Have a good time."

Denny smiled.

"We'll be back this afternoon sometime. That OK?"

Elliott nodded.

"Just come back safely."

And then she was gone. Opening the dark mahogany front door, walking across the stone flags of the courtyard, smiling as she saw Joaquim. For a moment, Elliott wondered if he should have allowed her to go. And then let the thought pass. She would be back. He left the window as the bike roared briefly before turning towards the road and the hills beyond.

The road took them past the grave. Even as they rounded the corner and began to coast down the long, uneven slope towards the barren farmlands below, Denny sensed the fear clutching at the edges of her mind.

This time, there was no woman. No cloaked figure. No shadow. Only the tall grasses moving, shuddering briefly as the wheels of the bike sprayed them with the dust and the grit of the road.

Joaquim stopped by the stone pillar, still leaning at an angle. He turned in his seat.

"You know what that is?"

Denny nodded.

"It's where the girl was buried."

"Not the girl," said Joaquim. "The lobisomen."

Denny got off the bike, shaking her head, throwing her long dark hair back over her shoulders. "I don't think so."

She had seen the goat, which was now walking slowly towards her, its head up, the small bell still hanging around its neck. Joaquim switched off the bike's engine, its low grumble giving way to the soft sound of the wind brushing across the dry ground and through the branches of the distant olive groves. There was no sign of the shepherd.

Denny knelt, stroking the goat as it stopped in front of her, running her hand down the side of its neck.

"They say it's her goat," said Joaquim.

"Whose?"

"The fishing girl. That he's waiting for her to come back."

Denny half-turned back towards him.

"Then it's a very old goat."

Joaquim smiled.

"Don't let him hear you say that."

"I don't suppose he'd understand."

"I think he might," said Joaquim switching on the bike's engine again, listening to the sudden burst of power. "Or maybe no one told you. The fishing-girl was English."

He had wanted to tell the girl.

As the shepherd had watched them pass, watched the dust, thrown up by the wheels of the bike, rise like smoke into the air behind it, before thinning and falling once again to the dry, pitted surface of the road, he had wanted to speak to the girl.

He could have waved to them. Shouted. Stopped them. But he hadn't. Preferring to keep his own counsel, leaning against the tall stick, his back to the sun, watching as the bike had turned towards the distant hills.

He knew that whilst the lobisomen still lived, the soul of the woman he had once loved would never be free. It had been a mistake to separate the urns. It had taken many years to realize, but it had been a mistake.

One had now been opened. The ashes it contained thrown to the winds, the creature it freed now living in the body of the woman who had scattered them. Soon, it would again attack the second one, the only other female in the family. To leave the body of the first and to take the soul of the second. *Que família nunca quer ter mais filhos.* So that the family would never have children again.

Already it had tried – in the cathedral, when the girls had stared at Elizabeth's gravestone and one had whispered the words, "In Spiritus". The creature had heard, rising from Hell through the ashes of the second urn. But the girl had escaped and her friend had died, protecting her. She had never been back and the spirit of the lobisomen would never stray far from the grave of its victim.

But now, whether by chance or by destiny, the girl was here. Prey to the lobisomen. The chance for the circle to be complete.

As much as he despised him, the shepherd knew that the monk was right. They had been given one last chance to burn the spirit of the creature for ever. And they must take it.

That was why he had not told the girl.

By the time they had reached the lower slopes of the hills, what little tarmac there had been on the road's surface had entirely disappeared, leaving only the natural shale and gravel of the earth's surface. Joaquim drove more slowly, working hard to control the rear wheel of the bike which continually threatened to skid to either side.

Denny hung on to him, the bag still over her shoulder bumping against her back as the bike clawed its way up the hillside. The sun was now high, burning the brown earth, its heat slowing the pace of all creatures below it, stilling any sense of movement. As they reached the skyline and paused, Denny looked back to the farmlands and coastline below them and it seemed to her as if all life had stopped. Caught in a moment of time and held for ever, like the twitch of a fly frozen between the two glass slides of a microscope.

"What happened to everyone?" she said. "Did the world just end and no one told us?"

Joaquim laughed.

"Nothing moves in the Algarve at midday. Except waiters."

He nudged the bike forward again, following a thin, almost invisible trail across the top of the hill. Up here there was a soft breeze, taking the edge off the sun's heat. It was coming off the land, blowing up the sides of the hills, cooling the small creatures that scrabbled through the dust looking for shade, and creating the currents of air that allowed the small flock of sequoia now above them to drift through the skies without movement.

Joaquim stopped the bike at the rise of the hill

before the track once again turned away and began to snake down towards the lifeless country below.

"OK, so nobody's doing anything, but it's a wonderful view."

Denny nodded.

The simple patchwork of the fields; their soft, muted colours. The dusty white scars across them that traced the paths and tracks worn by the people and the animals of a thousand years. The gun-metal sheen of the distant Atlantic. The dark swirl of the wetlands. The untidy, broad pockets of green fruit-trees. And, around and high above all, the rich, deep blue of the Algarvean skies that surrounded them, seeming to close out any sense of the rest of the world.

"The Moors called it Paradise," said Joaquim.

"I can believe it," said Denny.

Climbing off the bike, she sat down on the ground, swinging the bag from her shoulder, pulling out two cans of Coke.

"I'm afraid they'll be warm by now."

Joaquim smiled, sitting beside her.

"Then I'll ask the waiter to take them back."

They sat in silence for some minutes, gazing out at the land below them, sipping Coke. Denny had been right. It was warm. And flat.

"What's that?"

Denny was pointing down the hill, to the right.

Joaquim followed her gaze. She was looking at

jumbled piles of large stones, spread across the hillside, slowly being buried beneath thick, sprawling curls of ivy and the countless lichens and mosses left by the passing of the years.

"The monastery," said Joaquim. "Once upon a time it was supposed to have been something special but most of it fell over in the earthquakes." He crushed the empty Coke can in his hand. "You want to see it?"

"Is there anything to see?"

"No. Not really."

Denny stood up.

"Come on, then. Let's go and have a look at nothing."

There was no breeze as they neared the monastery, the only movement in the air caused by the exhaust of the bike as it crawled across the stony, pot–holed surface of what had once been an approach road.

Denny's attention had been taken by the small chapel, built into the side of the hill.

"That bit's still standing."

Joaquim turned the bike towards it, covering the ground slowly, hoping not to puncture either of the tyres. It would be a long walk home.

They stopped.

Denny slipped off the back of the bike and made her way carefully across the broken stones. They were hot. Their edges sharp. Joaquim stayed with the bike.

She was now close to the small chapel. The crumbling plasterwork. The wooden door that seemed cracked, broken. High above, the glass of the small windows that were shattered.

"Watch out for the monk!"

Denny turned quickly, half-expecting to see someone behind her. There was no one. Only Joaquim.

"What monk?"

Joaquim laughed.

"There's supposed to be a monk. He looks after the chapel."

Denny turned back to the small building.

"He doesn't seem to be doing it very well," she said.

It had been a long time since Joaquim had seen the monastery. As a boy, many years ago. The children of the local villages had always been told to stay away from the ruins. They were dangerous. There were ghosts. Rumours of the green mamba, a snake that killed brutally. *As cobras da serra*. The snakes that guarded the golden crosses of Santa Venezia, said still to be lying buried deep beneath the cold, dark stones.

There had only been three of them who had been brave enough to ignore the rumours and the warning. Or sufficiently foolish. It had also been a summer's day and, by the time they had walked up into the hills and finally found their way to the monastery, they had been far too tired to worry about any horrors that might await them. They had collapsed, exhausted, in the shade of a group of small pine trees, waking only as the sun had begun to sink towards the western skyline.

Joaquim put his hand to his forehead, shielding his eyes from the sun, looking for the trees.

He smiled. They were still there, a little way to the right of the chapel. And then the smile faded, his eyes narrowed and Joaquim's body was suddenly very still as he realized what was now standing in the shade of the dark, green trees.

The monk watched them as they walked slowly towards the trees. Peering through the broken glass of a small chapel window, his cold, grey eyes were unblinking. Like the snakes that haunted the sides of the hills around him.

"They have seen it."

The man standing in the shadows behind him nodded.

"I don't think it matters."

The monk turned away from the window, looking towards the man.

"When I want to know what you think, then I will tell you."

Joao nodded again. And was silent.

*　　*　　*

A cooling wind was blowing from the sea, damping down the heat of the late afternoon. Denny picked up her glass, drinking slowly.

There were few people in Jamie's Bar. Most had already left the beaches, retreating to the hotels and small guest-houses of the town, before wandering down the many side-streets in search of a restaurant for the evening.

They sat, looking out over the bay, where the waves of the afternoon had now flattened into a long, slow, rippling swell, washing the edges of the sand.

"Why were you frightened?" said Denny.

Joaquim paused for a moment.

"I don't know." He glanced at Denny. "Weren't you?"

"I didn't know what it was for."

Joaquim had been frightened of the cage since, at the age of seven, he'd first seen it. The thick, dark wooden bars, lashed together with rope. Rope that had first been soaked in the blood of a goat. The curling, cold steel of the hook, buried in its ceiling, from which they hung the body of the girl.

He had hidden behind his mother as the procession has passed by: the *mordomos*, stern-faced, carrying the cage, the body inside swinging from side to side like a corpse on a gibbet, turning in the wind.

Far from the sense of excitement, or even awe,

that his parents had expected of his first "procession", Joaquim's memories had been only of being buried in a jostling, sweating, agitated crowd. Of the smell of burning animal fat, drifting down from the torches that lit the way. Of the chorus of cheers that greeted the approach of the cage and of the screams of triumph as the body was finally lifted out and thrown on to the blazing fire.

He had been once. And had never gone again.

He picked up a small pebble and flicked it into the sand of the beach in front of them, shaking his head slowly.

"I hadn't expected to see it at the monastery."

Denny smiled.

"Maybe the monk looks after the cage as well."

7

The air was crisp. It wouldn't stay that way. All too soon the heat of the sun would smother the landscape, stifling thought and movement. But, as he rammed the jeep along the dusty track, Elliott was grateful for the cold draught of the early morning air that buffeted his face.

He always took the same route. Across the country. Avoiding the road. Since his wife had died, he had never used the carriageway. Never passed the corner where her car had left the road, the lonely curve that marked the highest point of the cliffs.

He spun the wheel, turning the car away from two gaunt, shaven sheep that had suddenly appeared on the track ahead. Neither of them had seemed to notice him, oblivious to the noise of the engine and intent only on scrabbling what nourishment they could from the dirt.

He had never known why Isobel had taken that road. It would have been out of her way. And no one knew how it happened. A farmer later said that he thought he had seen a woman walking along the side of the road but no one had ever come forward as a witness. There had not even been a body.

The car had fallen just over one thousand feet through the air before disappearing into the sea below. Some two days later, its shell had been dragged to the surface, its doors hanging open. Isobel had not been inside. Later, recording her death as "accidental", the coroner in Vilfeira had written that she had almost certainly been eaten by the sharks that were known to haunt that part of the coast. For very good reasons, it had not been a verdict that was widely reported.

Elliott stopped the jeep at some distance from the cliffs. The ground had begun to slope, swooping in a long, graceful curve towards the thin line that marked the limits of safety and the edge of the long drop to the waves below. Elliott was happy with his driving. He had less confidence in his brakes.

As he walked through the thick, wiry grass that clung to the drifting, sandy soil beneath, he looked north, along the line of the cliffs. The ribbon of the road was clear in the early morning sun. Deserted. Threading its way along the cliff-top, sometimes close to the edge, sometimes seeking safety in the contours of the barren land behind. His gaze fell on the tallest point, beneath which the dark waters of the Atlantic twisted and tumbled, each wave buckling against the impassive rock, each wall of spray reaching high into the air before falling back to welcome those that followed.

Elliott stood silently now, listening to the call of the gulls, watching, almost as if expecting to see his wife's car – waiting for it to spin off the road and trace long, slow cartwheels through the air, spinning noiselessly down towards the waters below.

But there was nothing. Just the lazy circles of the sequoia, turning slowly through the early morning sky.

Isobel had died on a Thursday. And each Thursday morning, in each week of the four years since her death, her husband stood, in memory of her, on the cliffs that marked her grave.

Denny sat alone in her bedroom. Upstairs. Away, now, from the shattered windows of the room below.

Downstairs, she could hear Lucilia pushing the stiff bristles of a house-brush across the cold stone of the floors. As she worked, Denny could hear her singing. Softly. Maybe it was the music of *fado*, the sad, lonely songs that reached to the very heart of the Portuguese soul and told of a world without hope and in despair. Elliott had described the Portuguese as being forever unhappy. As if a curse had been laid on them and never lifted.

There had to be exceptions, Denny thought, smiling gently. If there had been a curse, nobody ever seemed to have told Joaquim.

Except for yesterday. She had watched him as he had walked round the cage, seen the fear in his eyes. Maybe Joaquim was right. Maybe this procession was something to avoid like the plague.

She stood up.

Breakfast seemed a good idea. Orange juice. Perhaps one of the sweet-tasting bread rolls with cheese and cold tomatoes. Sliced. Eaten by the pool in the glow of the morning sun. Watching the curiously-coloured lizard make his first appearance of the day among the stones of the garden border. She'd asked Lucilia if it was dangerous. *Perigoso*. The maid had shaken her head, laughing quietly. There were no dangerous creatures in the Algarve. Maybe she didn't know about the snakes in the hills. Or the owls that flew into windows.

"*Bon dia*."

Denny smiled as she walked down the stairs, seeing Lucilia at the far side of the room.

"*Bon dia*, Lucilia. It's sunny again."

Lucilia nodded.

"Oh yes. *Sim. Muito calor*. Too hot. No good for working."

She wiped her hand across her forehead, suggesting, with a broad grin, that by half past nine, she was already washed out. Denny was wandering into the kitchen, her hand already reaching for the fridge door.

"How about a cold juice?"

Lucilia nodded vigorously.

"*Obrigada. Muito obrigada.*"

Denny poured two glasses. She put the kettle on, moved back into the wide, open-plan lounge, offering Lucilia the drink.

She sipped her own, listening to the chatter of the small birds in the trees outside and the slow, muffled wash of the sea along the edges of the beach.

Elliott's study door was open. He hadn't said so but Denny knew that it was probably somewhere that he preferred to be by himself. His retreat. His eyrie. She was curious. The kettle had begun to make its first sounds of life, the water slowly coming to the boil. She moved across the room, vaguely aware that Lucilia was watching her. But not caring.

Reaching the door, she grasped the handle, briefly thinking that she should do no more than pull it closed. But she went in.

The room was small. Sparsely furnished. A sofa. A rounded, mahogany table set against the wall with thin tapering legs reaching down to the flecked marble floor. A metal lamp, its base a broad, circular steel plate and its neck a tall stem that climbed toward the ceiling, before curving and swooping gracefully down to hold its head above the simple wooden desk.

Pens lay on the desk. Some jumbled papers. An open book. A clock in the shape of a horseshoe, whose slow tick seemed to fill the room. What noise there had been of the world outside seemed suddenly to have disappeared.

Denny moved slowly across the floor, her bare feet making no sound on the marble. Beside the clock, there was a photograph. Black and white. Held in a simple square silver frame. It was someone's face. Smiling. Denny moved closer, her gaze fixed now on the picture. Her heart had begun to quicken. She felt the pin-pricks running along the back of her neck. The sudden spike of fear that raced down her spine.

"Lucilia."

She muttered the word at first, almost as if afraid to make a noise. Then spoke it. And then screamed. The shriek of fear that now rang through the cold stone of the villa.

"Lucilia!"

The door opened, quickly. Sharply. The maid

now ran across the room, reaching for the girl, holding her, hugging her, whispering.

Slowly Denny calmed, dropping her head against the woman's shoulder, her breathing slowing, her tears no longer burning the corners of her eyes. Slowly, her mind came to terms with what she had seen. The face had been fatter. The hair healthier. The skin younger. The woman in the picture was smiling. And the woman in the picture had eyes.

But, in that moment, Denny had known that the woman in the picture was also the woman who was blind. And who had whispered the words, "In Spiritus".

She lifted her face towards Lucilia, her eyes once more welling with tears.

"Lucilia," she whispered. "Who's the woman in the photograph."

Lucilia looked down at the girl who lay in her arms, crying.

"That woman?"

She spoke slowly, aware of Denny's fear.

"Señorita, the woman in the picture . . . that was Señor Elliott's wife."

"She said what?"

Elliott dropped the keys to the jeep on to the plate glass of the dining table.

"That it was the same woman, señor. That the woman in the photograph—"

"She's ill."

Elliott walked quickly across the room, reaching the stairs, putting his hand briefly on Lucilia's shoulder as he passed her.

"But don't worry. It's probably no more than the heat."

Lucilia watched as he climbed the stairs, heard him as he quietly opened Denny's door.

Denny was asleep. Her head tilted to one side on her pillow, her breathing deep. The air in the bedroom was cool, the temperature kept low by the air-conditioning humming quietly in the background. Elliott walked slowly to her bedside, looking down at her. He picked up her hand, felt her wrist. The pulse beat seemed normal. He put his hand across her forehead. There was no obvious sign that Denny was ill. Lucilia had given her a small glass of brandy-mel, the local mixture of brandy and honey.

Elliott left the room, closing the door behind him. He walked down the stairs, began to cross the room.

"Is she. . .?"

"She's asleep," said Elliott, pausing and turning towards Lucilia. He smiled. "Maybe it's something to do with your local firewater."

Lucilia shrugged her shoulders. "Sometimes it helps."

"I'm sure it does." Elliott smiled again. "And it was a kind thought. *Obrigado*."

He carried on towards the study. He couldn't remember whether England was an hour in front. Or an hour behind. Or maybe it was neither. Maybe it was the same time among the rolling slopes of Weardale as it was on the dusty plains of Vilfeira. Summertime. The dog days.

He sat at the desk, reaching for the telephone, pulling it across the desk towards him. As he did so, he looked carefully at the picture of his wife. Smiling. Isobel. Whose body now lay on the shifting floor of the Atlantic and whose soul was now in Heaven.

Elliott's fingers began to punch at the numbered buttons. Then he stopped, listening for the sound of the phone ringing out in the hallway of Denny's home, in the distant corners of north-eastern England.

Isobel had stopped by the small shop window, her attention taken by a collection of rings. The dull lustre of the metal suggested that they were old. Some were plain, simply bands of stained silver; some broad, others thin, no more than narrow strands of wire. There were bigger ones – rings that boasted large, coloured stones: agate, jade, amethyst. None could be expensive. It was the kind of collection that might have grown with successive generations in even the humblest cottage on the Algarve, grown until the family had died out. Or perhaps simply grown tired of hoarding rings. And now they sat in a small shop window in a side-street of Vilfeira, gathering dust.

Isobel had gone in, listening to the bell click as she opened the door. It had long since lost the hammer that had once made it ring.

At first she had seen no one. The counter was bare but, at either side, deep shelves held out a bewildering, jumbled mixture of old clothes, ornaments, pictures and curios. Glass bottles of various shapes and sizes crowded the corner of one shelf and, on another, a large wooden elephant, missing one of its tusks, held its trunk aloft and seemed to bellow to the world at the indignity of such a loss.

Then, in the half-light of the small room, an old woman had appeared at the other side of the counter. Silently. As if having risen like a wraith from the floor.

"*Bon dia.*"

Isobel had smiled, turning quickly at the sound of the husky voice, almost surprised to find she was not alone in this strange world of glass bottles and proud elephants, frozen in time.

"*Bon dia, Señora*, I was looking at the rings. In the window."

The woman had nodded.

"*Momento, per favor.* I will find them."

And she had worked her way round the counter, moving to the window, pulling the faded, thick felt curtain to one side. She had leant over the various displays in front of her, reaching for the small wicker basket that held the rings.

"These?"

Isobel had nodded, smiling.

"Yes."

Like the cannibal proudly bearing the missionary's bloody head on a plate, the old woman had walked back across the room, holding the basket aloft, before finally leaving it on the counter in front of her first customer of the day.

"They are very pretty."

"They are," said Isobel, as she put her bag down on the counter and began to turn the rings over in her fingers. She had picked them up, one by one, holding them up against the light of the window.

"I think they are very old," the woman had said, hoping that a sense of age might add to their value. She had had no idea what they were worth. A farmer had called in one day, dropped them on the counter and said that since he and his family were moving from the area, they were trying to sell everything they didn't want to take with them. And that included the rings. The old woman had given him three thousand *escudos*. It had been nothing and both of them knew it. But neither had cared.

Isobel was now looking at a thick, heavy ring. It might have been gold. But it wasn't. The dull, dark yellow sheen was brass.

"How much for this?"

The old woman had shrugged, taken the ring and weighed it in her hand. She studied it carefully. The longer she took, the more she would ask. It was rounded, featureless, apart from the two letters crudely inscribed in its surface. "I.S." It might have been the name of the farmer.

"You want this?" she said at last, trying to disguise the tone of surprise in her voice.

Isobel smiled.

"I rather like it."

"For you?"

"I collect things."

"Then maybe you would also like this."

The old woman had given the ring back to her and disappeared into the small back room. Some minutes later, after the sounds of wooden boxes being repeatedly opened and shut suggested that she hadn't been immediately able to find her buried treasure, she had reappeared, holding a small pewter urn.

Isobel had taken it from her, running her fingers over the soft metal.

"Why this?"

"Look."

The shopkeeper had pointed to an inscription near its base.

"It's the same."

Isobel had lifted the urn, holding it up to what little light filtered in through the curtains that guarded the shop window. She had read the words aloud, slowly.

"I.S. In Spiritus."

Lowering it again, she had put it on the wooden counter.

"What does it mean?"

The old woman had shrugged her shoulders.

"I don't know."

"It's very pretty."

"It's very old."

Isobel slid the ring across the counter towards the small urn.

"How much for both of them?"

The shopkeeper had shrugged her shoulders again.

"I don't know. Four thousand, maybe?"

Isobel had reached into her bag, pulling out a slim leather wallet. She had given the old woman the four thousand–escudo notes. And then added five hundred. It was obvious that few customers found their way to this shop.

And she had turned, slipping the ring on to her finger, dropping the small urn in to her bag, saying thank you, and then she had noticed a picture, hanging at an angle on the wall beside the door.

Although the glass was cracked and its surface grimy, the colours of the picture beneath seemed to burn through the dirt. Isobel had walked up to it, peering at the scene, trying to understand it.

The figures seemed to be monks. They stood around a fire. A woman lay on the ground, her hands tied behind her back, her long black hair lying across the scorched earth, matted by the blood that ran from her face. One monk stood before her, a farmer's pitchfork held high above his head. And behind them stood a tall building, its massive arches and towers erupting from the hillside and reaching towards the deep blue corners of the Algarvean sky.

Isobel turned.

"Desculpe, Señora. . ."

The old woman had looked across from the window, where she was now folding the curtain back into its place, closing down the light from the street.

"This picture, what is it?"

The old woman had peered across the room. And then smiled.

"You have never heard of the lobisomen?"

"The what?"

"The lobisomen. Everyone in the Algarve has heard of this creature."

Isobel smiled.

"But I'm not from the Algarve. I'm from Lisbon."

"Ah."

The old woman nodded slowly, aware only of

Lisbon as a city many hundreds of kilometres to the north.

"Then perhaps you do not know. She was a witch. Hundreds of years ago. When they built the monastery in the hills. They killed her."

Isobel turned back to the picture.

"Who? The monks?"

The old woman grinned. She seemed to have lost all the teeth on her upper jaw.

"Yes, the monks. They burnt her. But first they put out her eyes."

"Look, she'll be fine."

Elliott heard his words echoing round the study as he spoke into the phone. Bouncing off the glass of the tall windows and the bright surface of the marbled floor.

"I don't know what's wrong. I think it's probably the heat. Most of the time she seems perfectly happy and I find myself thinking that it was absolutely the right thing to do to have her staying here. Away from it all. Where there's nothing at all to remind her of what happened. And, right out of the blue, she seems to have these nightmares. . . No . . . no, she's asleep at the moment. Lucilia gave her something, I don't know, some kind of local magic. . . Who? She's the maid. She comes and helps me twice a week. Sometimes more if she feels like it. . . I don't know. Maybe we should give Denny time. She's already made a friend. Joaquim. Seems pleasant enough. He works at a local beach bar and if she's got someone of her age to talk to, rather than some old fool like me all the time, then I think we've probably seen the worst of it. Time, Richard. It's a great healer."

When he had finished the call, Elliott slowly put the receiver back on the set, thinking of his brother in England. He too had lost his wife. Many years before. Now Denny was all that he had. All that any of them had. The only girl, the only woman left in the family. And what he had told Denny of the lobisomen, as they had walked in the wetlands, had crept into the edges of his mind. But it was nonsense. A story to frighten children. In the real world, it had been a friend of Denny's who had died.

Which was why it had to be better for Denny to be enjoying the sunshine of the Algarve, the colours, the smells and the sense of holiday. Rather than sitting by the side of a newly dug grave in southern Ireland, under the leaden grey skies of the summer.

The green BMW had been parked in the town square. Isobel had left the windows open, hoping that the slight breeze coming off the sea would make the car less like an oven when she got back to it. Cars were rarely stolen in Vilfeira.

The February sunshine was warm. It would be a long summer.

Had Jamie's Bar been open, she might have called by for a spritzer, a long cold drink of light *vinho verde*, Portugal's famous "green" wine, mixed with chilled mineral water. After the dusty side-streets of the town, it would have been welcome. But Jamie's wouldn't open until Easter. Some six weeks away. Isobel had smiled, thinking that she couldn't wait that long and would treat herself instead to a long slow drive along the cliffs, where the brilliant yellow mimosa, buttercups and celandine would be in full bloom, layered across the grasses and thin hedgerows. Where she could walk and feel the sting of the Atlantic spray in her face and watch the gulls spinning and calling to each other as Spring edged closer.

But there had been no gulls that morning.

Leaving Vilfeira, she had driven up to the headland that overlooked the town and then turned right, heading north. The road had been deserted. As she had climbed higher and higher above the town, she had stopped, getting out of the car to look back over the plains of Vilfeira beyond the soft, pink roofs of the town. Briefly, in the early spring, the countryside buried its barren earth beneath a sea of almond blossom, the brilliant pink and white flowers of the trees stretching across the fields and wastelands like confetti, blown by the wind.

The cloths of Heaven.

The words of Yeats had come back to her, so many years after first reading them at school. She had sat by the car, letting the view before her soak to the very edges of her mind. She would force herself to remember it when the long, hot, summer days had turned the grassy slopes to a wasteland and the thick, moist earth into dust.

And she had taken out the small pewter urn. Opening it, for the first time, she had been surprised to find that it was filled with sand.

Pouring it into her hand, looking more closely, she had then realized that it was not sand. That what she was holding were the ashes of a fire. That what she had bought might have been the funeral urn of someone long dead.

And she had stood up, gazing out over the brilliant flowers of the cliffs and the long sweeping blossoms of the almond trees across the plains below. She had thrown the ashes into the wind, letting them scatter beneath the blue skies of the Algarve. As she did so, she had blessed them with two words.

"In Spiritus."

And then she had turned away, looking up the road ahead, getting back into the car. She thought she saw someone, walking, in the distance. Perhaps she could offer them a lift.

As she had drawn closer, she could see now that

it was a woman, her shoulders hunched, a black shawl pulled over her head, a long black dress that reached to the ground and dragged in the dust of the roadside. Isobel had slowed, stopping beside the figure.

"Can I help you?"

A thin white hand had reached down, pulling open the door. Slowly the woman had lowered herself into the car, her shoulders and face turned away from Isobel. Her clothes were old, smelling of the dried grease of animals and the pungent, acrid smoke of a campfire.

She closed the door.

Moving into first gear, Isobel had started the car forwards again, the engine straining slightly as they wound their way up towards the highest point of the cliffs. A slow, right-hand bend that curled towards the sea and then back toward the shelter of the land.

Isobel had turned to her passenger.

"There's a lovely view from up here."

Still the woman did not speak. Perhaps she was frightened. Perhaps she thought Isobel was driving too quickly.

The white hand was now reaching out, moving towards Isobel, touching the ring on her finger. The corner was now coming up fast, the road levelling as it reached the top of the cliff. The woman's head was now turning slowly. Isobel found herself looking at her, ignoring the road. The car engine had begun to race. Now the woman's face stared at Isobel, the thin white cheeks, the almost transparent skin stretched over the bones, the hoarse, rasping voice that whispered "In Spiritus" and the deep, bloody hollows that had once been her eyes. Isobel gripped the wheel, the car slewed off the road, its wheels now tearing at the grasses. She hammered her foot on the brake, skidding across the ground, her eyes still fastened on the woman's face that was now leaning towards her, the mouth opening, the yellow claws of her teeth bared, the rancid smell of her breath hot on Isobel's face, the thin white hands clutching at her throat. Isobel had screamed and then fallen silent as the mouth had closed on her neck.

There had been no cries from the gulls as the car had finally plunged over the edge of the cliffs and fallen through the air, its open doors flapping as, in its final moments, the strangled chicken jerks its wings before a painful death.

And no sound from the sequoia that floated in the deep blue sky above.

8

Many of the coffins had rotted over the years. As he moved amongst them, holding the lantern above his head, the monk would look down and see the bones of bodies that had been dead for centuries now protruding through the crumbling wood. Many had simply been left on the cold, stone floor. Others had been lifted into hollows chiselled out of the rock of the walls. These had been the "fathers". *Los pais*. The elders of the community, those who had earned a place in the catacombs of the hills rather than in the dirt of the plains below.

The air was cold. Deep in the shadows he could hear the gentle splashing of the stream that ran through the caves. The same stream that, many years before, had carried away the blood of those whom the monks had wished to free. Those whose limbs had to be broken. Those who had died in agony long before they could be burnt. Those whose bones would hang on the walls of the chapel. He was now past the coffins and found himself standing at the edge of the chamber.

Before the earthquakes, broad stone steps had led from the monastery down to this cave. In the villages of the plains below, they would joke that this was where the monks had kept their wine, which was why the stream was sometimes red as it seeped out of the hillside and into the dust. They knew it wasn't true. Many times, they had woken to hear the screaming deep into the night. But still they told the joke.

The ceiling of the chamber was high, bending in a wide dome across the even, stone floor. Natural light filtered in through a crack that ran for much of its length, allowing the monk to lower his lantern and set it down on the ground. The steps had long gone, buried beneath the tons of rubble that had been the earthquake's legacy. Now the only entrance was through the catacombs, past the coffins and the rotted corpses of the fathers.

It would be sufficient.

The monk had seen the instruments many times before. Often he would clean them, lacquering them with a fine, light yellow oil, spreading it across the blades, the claws and the sharpened, glittering needles. Now they hung silently from the wooden beam that stretched above the tables, turning in the dull gleam of the lantern.

The three tables were made of stone. Each with the leather buckles that would hold the body in place, gripping it by the wrists and ankles, spreading it across the table's width. It was said that when all three tables screamed, the sound was heard in the furthest corners of Heaven. And in the darkest pits of Hell.

The monk had heard the screams. Often in his sleep, he had listened to the agonized shrieks of the innocent, silenced only by the pitiless rasp of the saw. And he had woken, sweating, the sound weeping from the walls of rock about his bed. And he had lain awake until the first glimmers of dawn, wondering if he would be strong, should he ever be called.

And now, very soon, he would know.

He picked up the lantern once more, walking slowly towards the tables. He stopped by the first one, his hands reaching down, touching its smooth, cold surface. Running his fingers over the hard, unyielding leather of the buckle. His gaze moved upwards, towards the head of the table. Towards the letters carved in the stone.

Letters that would be finally burnt into the skin. Letters that had once haunted each soul on the plains of the Algarve but which had for two hundred years been forgotten. Letters that the monk now whispered to himself.

"I.S."

He nodded slowly, almost as if in prayer.

"In Spiritus."

The words and their meaning known only to the monks of Santa Venezia. The words that would conjure up the spirit of the lobisomen. In time.

He turned, carrying the lantern aloft once more, walking back towards the coffins and the sleeping ghosts of the fathers.

"How is she?"

Joaquim had left his bike leaning against the tall carob tree that, in the sunshine of the late afternoon, now threw its shadow across the wooden slats of Emilio's garden shed. He was smiling as Elliott opened the villa's front door.

"How did you know?"

"Lucilia. She's my aunt. In Portuguese, *Tia. Tia Lucilia.* Sounds OK, yes?"

Elliott smiled. Amongst the small communities of the Algarve, everyone claimed to be related to everyone else.

"You didn't come into Jamie's today, so I phoned her."

"Were you expecting us?"

"Denny said she'd persuade you."

Elliott laughed. Then stood to one side of the door.

"Come in. But I don't know if she's awake."

Lucilia hadn't told Joaquim about the photograph. Simply that Denny had fainted. That it was probably the heat.

"Shall I. . . ?"

Joaquim hesitated, pausing in the centre of the lounge. Elliott began to climb the stairs, turning back towards him.

"I'll ask her to join you outside. And have a drink. There's some cans in the fridge."

Joaquim smiled and wandered into the kitchen, taking out a Coke, snapping it open and drinking deeply. Jamie's had been hard work today. He was pleased it was over.

He walked back through the house and out on to the veranda, looking out over the bay. In the distance, Vilfeira was already beginning to disappear into the blue shadows thrown over the town by the headland and cliffs behind it. The sea was calm, quieter now at the approach of the evening.

"Hi."

Joaquim turned. Denny was standing behind him, leaning against the glass doors of the veranda. She was smiling. Joaquim took a step towards her.

"I heard you were—"

"I'm fine," she said, coming forward now and kissing him lightly on the cheek. "But it was kind of you to drop by."

They sat at the round wooden table and,

throwing a towel over his arm, Elliott played waiter, bringing them crisps and small cheese-biscuits from the kitchen. And a delicately hand-painted bowl, filled with glistening, light green olives.

"And I'm sorry but we're right out of burnt sardines."

Elliott bowed and smiled, then said he had work to do. He did not add the words "in the study".

Beneath the veranda, a small brightly coloured lizard had appeared, making its way through the stiff, dried grass of the lawn, its legs moving slowly, its head held high. Imperious. Proud. Afraid of nothing, until Denny stood up and walked to the edge of the veranda, leaning over the low wooden rail to study the creature more closely. It stared hard at her at first and then turned, chasing furiously across the grass, seeking safety finally among the cracks and shadows of the stones bordering the garden.

The sides of the hills were burnished by the deep gold of the setting sun as it dropped slowly through the western skies. For the villagers of the plains below, it meant the close of the day. A cold beer by the back door of the cottage. The smell of woodsmoke. The taste of chicken burnt slowly over the white-hot embers of a charcoal fire.

For men such as those who now stood outside the chapel door, it was a way of life. A simple, uncomplicated way of life. One that had been handed down through successive generations. One that belonged to the hunter-gatherers of pre-history who killed for their supper. And one that belonged to Moorish poets who had once sat by camp-fires in the Algarve and conjured up wild tales of fabled creatures and whimsical stories of romance.

Of the king who had planted almond trees throughout the countryside so that, in Springtime, as their white blossom covered the earth, so his Norwegian queen would think herself at home again, surrounded by the snows of her homeland. Of the cannibal giants who waited for sailors unlucky enough to fall off the edge of the world. And of the witch with the teeth of a wolf who ran screaming through the night, tearing out the throats of her victims and feasting on their souls.

The men were waiting for the monk. Thirteen. The *mordomos*. He had called them for sunset, caring little that their long walk home would be in darkness.

"I should be going."

Joaquim glanced at his watch. Half past six. By half past seven it would be dark, and he knew his mother was alone.

"What does your father do?"

As they sat, watching the sun fall behind the

distant headland, picking at the olives in the thin, blue bowl, Denny thought how very little she knew about Joaquim's family. Or even about Joaquim. A boy. A young man. With ambitions, one day, to be a lawyer. Happy, for the moment, to while away the long summer in Jamie's Bar. The doors of the University of Coimbra, four hundred miles to the north, would not open again until October.

"Joao? During the summer he cuts cork. In winter he's a painter."

Denny looked across at him.

"A painter? As in Picasso?"

Joaquim laughed.

"No. As in *Joao Placido Correia*. Painter and decorator of houses, doors and chimney pots."

He took another olive, holding the fruit in his fingers, watching its damp skin glisten in the evening sunshine.

"I think he might have once wanted to be an artist. When he was younger. I don't know. He doesn't very often talk about it." He lifted the olive slowly to his mouth. "I suppose we can all dream."

The lizard had reappeared, lifting its head above the rocks of the garden, hungry for the small insects that the evening would bring.

"And you?" said Denny.

Joaquim looked back at her.

"Me?"

"What do you dream of?"

For a moment Joaquim said nothing. He took the olive stone from his mouth, knowing that Denny was asking about his future but conscious now only of the present picture in his mind. The young girl who spoke to him but whose words could not be heard.

"She is saying something."

Joaquim's voice was quiet.

"Who is?" said Denny, surprised by the change in tone.

"The girl I see in my dreams," said Joaquim slowly. "Each night she has been there. Each night she is saying something. One word. But I can't hear her. Her mouth is opening but I can't hear the words. And I want to talk to her, to ask her . . . but she goes away, walking slowly down a road, waving goodbye."

He stopped, the image clear in his mind.

It wasn't a road he knew. Nor had he ever seen the tidy green fields that lay at either side. Or the church that stood beyond them. And it was raining, yet the roadside flowers were in full bloom. In the Algarve, it rained only in winter and, in winter, the flowers of the Algarve are dead.

The man with the scar on the back of his hand had said nothing. Whilst the monk had quietly explained what had to be done, he had stood with his back to the setting sun, his eyes on the ground, his long shadow reaching across the stones.

Others had spoken. Joao had asked why it had to

be this way. The monk had spat on the ground, as if in contempt. There was no other way. And Joao had then fallen silent and spoken no more.

The monk had shown them the snakes.

The long, thin green water-snakes that had once curled through the ditches of the wetlands but which now moved silently through the waters of the well and of the streams that trickled quietly into it. Snakes that the monk had pulled from the water with his hands and held high in the air as they writhed and twisted in his grasp. Snakes that he had held in the faces of the men who stood before him, showing them the greedy black eyes, the flickering tongues, the opened mouths and curling fangs that drove poison into the blood of their prey.

Death from the bite was slow, painful. The muscles would stiffen, each one twisting against the bone, tightening, as if pressed in a vice. Slowly, the poison would burn its way through the stomach, the lungs, the throat and the edges of the brain, causing the final agony that brought madness. A madness that drove victims of the snakes to thrash wildly in the dirt, clutching their own bodies, tearing at them as if in hope of dismemberment and thus the end of pain. And, in that final madness, as the red mist burnt in their eyes, the victims died. This, the monk had said, would be their reward. If they refused.

But he knew they would not.

Even the man with the scarred hand, who had not looked at the monk, had not moved at the sight of the snakes and had not spoken. Even he had finally nodded his head, slowly, turning away and then walking with Joao as the men began their journey back to the villages below.

They had walked in silence. Each man buried in his own fears. Each knowing that nothing could, or ever would, be said.

Above them, the early evening stars sparkled in the silent skies of the Algarve and, amongst the trees, the genet and the mongoose moved quietly in search of their prey.

9

She could see its head quite clearly.

In the early morning, peering out from the dark shadows of its home among the rocks, the lizard was taking its first look at the day. Listening for the unwelcome footstep. Watching for the first insects to crawl within its reach.

Denny sipped her coffee, leaning back in the wooden garden chair, her gaze firmly fixed on the creature. At one side of the gardens, she could hear Emilio still chopping wood. It seemed odd that anyone would want wood in the middle of summer. Lucilia had had simply shaken her head and thrown her hands into the air when Denny had pointed towards him. And then drawn a line across her forehead. It wasn't entirely clear but, as she'd walked into the morning sunshine of the garden, Denny had smiled. It didn't take a genius to work out that Lucilia wasn't too impressed by Emilio's skills as a gardener.

The lizard was now in the open, stretching on the grass, letting the sun wash the richly-coloured patterns of its back. Denny wondered if it could see her. Earlier, she had left small crumbs of bread among the blades of grass, wondering if the creature would find them. Or, even if it did, whether or not it would eat them.

It now stretched out a front leg, slowly pulling itself forward, almost as if in imitation of a chameleon. Denny had decided that the animal should be called Tim. Years ago, there had been a goldfish called Tim. A golden, slow-moving creature that she'd won at a fair, throwing tennis balls into large, wooden barrels. Even for a ten year-old it had been easy, and Denny had said that it was almost as if the man running the stall had been trying to get rid of his goldfish.

Then Leyla had tried. And missed with every ball.

The lizard was now moving through the grass. Haphazardly. Turning at once this way and then that. Padding forwards quickly and then stopping suddenly, its head erect, its body stiff, its small black eyes staring, unblinking, at the shapes and colours of the world around it.

And Denny smiled.

Leyla would have found some way of talking to the small creature. Some means of winning its attention and conjuring up a wild and rambling conversation about life as a lizard. For Leyla, the world had never been anything more than a huge, if sometimes mysterious, joke. A place in which you might as easily talk to a lizard as stumble across the pot of gold at the foot of a rainbow. A life that no one was expected to take too seriously and one whose meaning lay at the heart of the sound of laughter.

Denny had rarely seen her friend without a broad smile on her face or that infectious sparkle in her eyes.

Until at last she had seen her falling through the air. Spinning over and over, slowly, almost as if floating, her outline and shadow becoming smaller as she drew further away, her body twitching before finally driving into the ground, where her bones had broken on the cold marble of the cathedral floor.

Since then, there had been little laughter.

Emilio had stopped chopping the wood and was now walking across the gardens towards the villa. He walked slowly, the short, stubby axe hanging from the fingers of his right hand, while, with his left, he rubbed the sweat from his forehead.

The lizard was staring at Denny, bringing her back from the memories of a cold April afternoon, when the grey north-eastern skies had hung low over the glistening Durham rooftops and a fine rain had been spitting in her face as she watched the body of her friend being carried out through the tall, wooden cathedral doors.

From the kitchen she could hear Lucilia singing. A tuneless, repetitive song that that seemed at odds with the bright colours of the morning and with the curious, almost humorous way in which the lizard was now cocking its head to one side, as if trying to see if Denny might appear different if she was looked at sideways.

Denny whistled softly. Then began to make a low clicking noise with her tongue.

At first, the creature seemed uninterested. Or deaf. But then, slowly, its head straightening, its eyes still on the girl, it began to move forwards again, its attention taken by the sound. The muscles of its body rippled gently as it moved, the brilliant yellow diamonds of its back shimmering across the pale blue leather of its skin.

Neither had seen Emilio.

The gardener had stopped and was now watching them, quietly, moving his arm slowly. The lizard took another step towards Denny. She clicked her tongue again. And then saw the movement in the corner of her eye. She swung her head towards the gardener, grabbing the arms of the chair, pulling herself up.

"No!"

The word caught in her throat, the muscles of her neck suddenly tight, her scream cut short by the sudden blur of the hand, the glitter of the axe-blade spinning viciously through the air and the sickening, brutal snap as it buried itself in the ground, cutting the animal's body in half.

And in the kitchen Lucilia still sang. Quietly.

Emilio began to walk across the grass, his eyes on the small, broken body of the lizard. Reaching it, kneeling now in front of Denny, he stretched out his hand, towards the wooden axe-handle.

"No!"

Denny screamed at the man. He stopped. His hand still touching the axe, his head slowly turning towards her.

"Leave it! Leave it where it is!"

Emilio, still kneeling, was now looking across his shoulder at Denny.

"*E horrivel*," he said slowly.

"I don't understand!" shouted Denny. "You get it? I don't understand!"

Emilio looked back to the axe and, putting his fingers round its handle, began to pull it out of the ground. The lizard's body lifted with it, as if stuck to the metal by the blood that quickly congealed in the glare of the Algarvean sun.

Denny stood silently watching him. Suddenly, she was feeling foolish. Maybe '*e horrivel*' meant

dangerous. Or even poisonous. Maybe she owed
the man.

She watched as he walked to the bushes at the
edge of the lawn and threw the pieces of the lizard's
body deep amongst them. Maybe it had even been a
lizard that had scarred the back of his hand.

"*Disparate! Idiota!*"

Sofia threw the plate on the table. Joao said
nothing, waiting for his wife to calm. The cheese
that had been on the plate had fallen on the floor.

"It's crazy! The man's mad!"

Still Joao said nothing.

Many years before, when they had first married,
Sofia had been happy for him to join the *mordomos*. It
would be an honour, she had said, to be the wife of
one of the carriers in the procession. Who knows?
One day they might make him mayor. She had never
taken it too seriously, preferring to think of it only as
some kind of men's drinking club. An excuse to get
together over bottles of beer and *medronho*.

She knew about the monk. The strange little
man with greasy hair who led the procession each
year. The man with blue eyes that stared into the
darkness and then into the brightest flames of the
fire. She knew they went to see the monk.
Whenever he rang the bell.

And she knew that they had climbed up into the
hills to see him the night before. That they had

returned to the nearby villages after dark. And that Joao and Emilio had sat long into the night, talking in low voices, smoking heavily.

And, as she had lain in her bed, waiting for her husband, so she had begun to listen to their conversation, their tongues loosened, as midnight drew close, by the glasses of *medronho*. As she had listened, so she had slowly begun to realize that the reality of what she had once thought of as no more than a game for the men of the villages, a happy diversion from their drab, repetitive days, was no less than a blood-line stretching back to the slaughters of the past.

"You're all mad! And don't think—"

"Woman!"

Joao stood up, throwing his chair across the room, hammering it against the white stone wall.

"You should never have listened!"

"Thank God that I did!"

Sofia gripped the edges of the table, the veins in her arms twitching beneath the surface of her skin, her eyes red from the tears of the morning. Tears that had burnt at the edges of her eyes. Tears that she could share with no one. Except Joao.

"We must be rid of the lobisomen!"

"Dear God. . ." Sofia now fell slowly to the floor, tears once more beginning to run down her pale cheeks. "Don't you understand, Joao. There's no such thing as the lobisomen. It's an old story."

Joao didn't move, watching as his wife pulled the edges of her dress to her eyes, wiping them slowly.

"But the monk. . ."

"Joao, the monk's a madman. He lives alone in the hills. His brain's gone." She looked up at her husband. "Can't you see that?"

Joao now moved round the table, kneeling by his wife's side, reaching out his arm and putting it around her shoulders. She was warm, her skin moist.

"I'm sorry."

Sofia looked up at him, the lines of his forehead deep, where once there had been a clear, tanned skin. She reached out her hand, stroking it across the grey stubble of his chin.

"You don't have to do this, Joao."

"But. . ."

"Dear God, please."

Joao leant forwards, kissing his wife gently on her cheek. And then stood, turned away and, reaching into his pocket for his cap, walked quickly through the small, open door at the front of the cottage and out into the bright sunlight of the early afternoon.

It was much later that Joaquim found his mother. He'd come home from Jamie's for a new shirt. A child had spilt orange juice over the one he had been wearing.

She had been lying on the floor, in front of the small unlit fire. She had been asleep and yet

114

Joaquim had seen the stains of the tears down the sides of her face. He had touched her forehead softly. It had been hot.

And he had woken her and helped her to her bedroom. Made her a cold drink. Settled her on her bed, all the while saying nothing. And later, as the shadows of the afternoon began to lengthen and the small birds in the branches of the almond tree outside began to chatter at the prospect of the day's end, so Sofia had finally told him. Speaking softly, the tears once more in her eyes, she talked of the monk, of the procession and of what the men would do.

And Joaquim had listened. And then knelt down to pray.

Manuel kept to the side streets.

He rarely came into Vilfeira, preferring to live his life among the tanglewood and dust of the countryside, where the world moved slowly and without noise. Sometimes his wife would ask him to come with her and they would clamber aboard the squat, rusting bus that blundered along the country tracks each morning on its daily visit to the town.

Today, he was alone. Later, when it was evening, Manuel would take the bus home. After his visit to the *esquadra da policia*, the small, concrete building in the Rua das Armadas, a street running off the town square.

Twice he took the wrong turning, wandering down the almost deserted streets, staying close to the walls, as if afraid that he would be seen. He had told no one he was coming.

When, at last, he found the square, he walked quickly down its side, keeping his eyes from the tall pile of wood that stood at its centre. The fire that, on Saturday, as darkness fell, would be lit to burn the lobisomen.

The Rua das Armadas was a thin, cobbled street. Hidden from the sun of the late afternoon by the tall buildings that surrounded the square, Manuel felt almost comfortable in its shadowed silence. The soft leather soles of his boots moved quietly over the cobbles, the few coins in his pockets jingling softly as he now quickened his pace, wiping his brow with his cap, spitting on the stones to rid his throat and lungs of the dust that hung in the foetid air.

The *esquadra da policia* was no more than an open door, two small shuttered windows at either side and a small, blue, metal notice, hanging lopsidedly on the wall, on which the word "*Policia*" had once been enamelled. Now the letters were barely visible, much of the enamel having been worn away by car fumes and the heat that seemed to eat into the very fabric of the town's buildings.

Manuel paused at the door.

When he had first become a *mordomo*, he had

sworn on the soul of his mother that he would keep the faith. That the secrets handed down over the centuries of the brotherhood of the monastery of Santa Venezia da Vilfeira would be his to share, but never his to tell. And he had watched as the monk had slit open the belly of the snake and pulled out its heart, to then hold it out in the palm of his hand, inviting Manuel to eat. To show faith.

He walked through the door, his eyes having to adjust to the shadows of the room he found himself in. He was aware of the man in the corner. Sitting quietly, not moving. Watching Manuel. Smoke from his cigarette hung in the air. Manuel turned.

"*Boa dia.*"

The man said nothing.

"I have come. . ."

Now the man stood up, walking slowly across the room, his face shadowed, his eyes hidden behind dark sunglasses.

"Who are you?"

The voice was hard, unemotional.

"My name is Manuel Pereira. A *mordomo.*"

In the street outside, a small boy's voice could be heard calling for his mother. The child called out twice. And then was silent. Manuel could smell the man's breath. The tobacco, the lingering traces of sweetened brandy. Somewhere in the room an electric fan was turning slowly, moving the air and the curls of blue smoke that drifted through it.

"And what do you want? Manuel Pereira."

Manuel could feel the blood beginning to pump violently through his heart. The familiar pains were coming back. The pains that had killed his father. The pains that would one day kill him.

"I. . ."

He hesitated. He had eaten the snake's heart. He had sworn on the soul of his mother. They would find out. They would know. One day. Surely.

"The procession. . ." he began. And then stopped.

Still the fan purred in the background. Still the man in front of him said nothing, staring impassively through black glasses, letting the smoke of his cigarette drift from the edges of his mouth and soak into the thick matted hair of his broad moustache.

Manuel held his hands together, his head bowed, as if in apology. Then the policeman spoke again, the low, harsh voice seeking out each fear Manuel had thought hidden in the corners of his mind.

"Tell me about the procession. Manuel Pereira."

Joaquim stood in the middle of the road, watching as his father walked towards him. Joao looked tired. The day had been hot and stripping the bark from the cork oak trees had stretched the muscles of his body to their limits. A dull, crippling pain now ran down the length of his spine, a pain that could be partially relieved only by dropping his shoulders, by stooping, by leaning forward as he walked.

Joaquim wondered briefly how much longer his father would work the fields. Many had died, much younger than Joao. The body aged quickly beneath the sun of the Algarve.

"*Boa tarde*."

Joao stopped in front of his son, his dulled, grey eyes meeting Joaquim's gaze. He nodded briefly in reply.

"*Boa tarde*."

"Is it true?"

Joaquim watched his father carefully, knowing that the older man would ignore the question.

"I'm tired," said Joao.

"Mama told me."

Joao stiffened, his flickering eyes suddenly still.

"And you. . .?"

"No."

Joaquim waved his hand briefly.

"No. I haven't told anyone."

Joao nodded. Then started walking again, moving to one side of the narrow, broken road to avoid his son. Joaquim made no attempt to stop him.

"But, is it true?"

Again the question. Again no reply from his father. And then.

"It's nothing. *Nada*. It's all nonsense."

Joaquim turned, watching as Joao began to move away from him towards the village where the setting sun now washed the small, hunched white cottages with the brilliant orange colours of the early evening.

"I need to know, Papa."

Joao stopped, turning slowly round to face his son.

"No, Joaquim. No, you don't."

"Priest!"

The captain had climbed out of the car and was now walking across to the small chapel. At his back, the evening sun was dropping slowly through the sky towards the distant, rolling waters of the Atlantic, closing the day and ushering in the uncertainties of the night. Manuel had felt sure that he must speak. That he must tell someone. But now, as the light began to ebb from the skies and as he watched the policeman hammering on the chapel doors, he was suddenly afraid.

The doors opened.

Manuel could see the monk, his face turned upwards towards the tall figure of the captain. He was nodding, listening. Then he looked towards the car and the pains returned to Manuel's body. Even though, at this distance and in the shadowed light of the evening, it was difficult to see the man's face, Manuel could yet feel the stony, dull glare of the blue eyes reaching deep down into his soul.

He had broken the code. Broken faith.

The man would surely be arrested and thrown behind the stiff, ramrod bars of the *esquadra*'s small jail, yet still Manuel cowered before the monk's gaze. Even though the man was no more than a clown. An idiot with a line in magical tricks. An imposter. It had all been no more than a game.

But then the rules had changed.

The police captain had turned away and was walking back towards the car. The monk was nowhere to be seen.

Manuel frowned. Perhaps the captain had not believed him. Perhaps the monk had told him a string of lies. That he, Manuel, was playing games. It was possible. After all, they'd all been taken in. Emilio. Joao. The old man. All of them. The brave *mordomos*. The puppets of a madman dressed up as a monk.

"Get out."

The captain had pulled the door open. At first, Manuel didn't move, unsure of what was happening.

"Out!"

The captain's hand reached into the car, grabbing Manuel by the collars of his crumpled, dirty shirt and dragging him out. Manuel heard the material tear.

"Idiot! *Seu burro!*"

The captain's voice was low, ill-tempered. He spat the word into Manuel's face.

"But, Señor, I. . ."

"Tell it to the priest!"

"But it's true!"

The policeman threw Manuel on to the ground, swinging his boot, kicking him unmercifully in the ribs. Manuel screamed, clutching his arms to the top of his chest, rolling into a ball. He felt the pain at the side of his head, the boot-heel hard against his spine. Felt the blood begin to trickle from the edges of his mouth. And then lay quite still, breathing hard, soaking up the pain that twisted through his body. He heard the car engine cough into life. The squeal of tyres on the hard gravel of the track and the sound of the car receding into the distance.

And then all was still again. Quiet, save for the evening wind that blew softly up the sides of the hills and the sound of a sea-bird calling through the skies above, as the sun slowly settled behind the surface of the sea.

"So, *compinxa*. You would have betrayed us all."

The monk's voice was slow, deliberate. Manuel did not look up.

"The captain is a greedy man. He is also very stupid. Like you."

Manuel said nothing, his arms folded tightly across the broken bones of his chest.

"He thinks I know where the five crosses are hidden. The five crosses of Santa Venezia. Like all peasants, he believes the stories."

The monk spat on the ground.

"But he is a fool. There are no crosses. No gold. But he believes the stories and he is greedy."

The monk stared impassively at Manuel, lying in the dust at his feet, his face twisted in pain. He wondered if the man could even hear him.

"So I tell him that I can show him the gold. But only if he leaves the procession alone. No matter what happens, he must leave it alone. And I promise him the gold to make sure that he doesn't listen to fools like you."

The monk smiled.

"It was a secret. Between the captain and me. And now he's angry because he says you'll open your stupid mouth and ruin everything. *Cabrao!* You were unlucky. You told the wrong person. I told him he should kick you till your bones broke."

Still Manuel did not look up. His eyes were open but he saw little. Only the red mist that swam before them, slowly clearing.

"Instead, he has left you to me."

He felt the monk's hand take his arm and pull him unsteadily to his feet. He could smell the thick, heavy garlic of the man's breath. The stench of clothes that had been worn unwashed. He felt himself being pushed forwards, each painful step taking him closer to the edge of the hills, where the wind blew.

Finally he was left to stand alone. Rocking slightly, his balance uncertain, the red before his eyes now thinning. He could not see what the monk was wrapping round his neck. It felt cold. Like a rope. Except that it seemed to be alive. As if the rope had muscles which now rubbed against his skin.

He opened his eyes wide, the final traces of the red mist of blood that had covered them disappearing, letting Manuel briefly glimpse the greedy black eyes of the snake before it opened its thin jaws and sank its long, curving teeth into the side of his face.

And the monk laughed as he kicked the screaming man and the snake coiled about his neck over the edge of the hill, watching him tumble crazily, like a rag doll, down the stony side towards the evening shadows of the country plains far below.

10

As he rode his bike slowly through the early morning, Joaquim knew it had to be nonsense.

No sane person would ever do what his mother had heard them talking about. They must have been drunk. When he'd seen him on the road the night before, Joaquim had thought that his father looked dreadful. *Medronho.* Too much of it, sitting beneath the stars at midnight, both he and Emilio inventing more and more lurid stories.

By the time he reached Jamie's, leaning his bike against the slatted wooden walls at the back of the small building, Joaquim knew that it had all been no more than the boasting of older, drunken men. Who should have known better. He was annoyed that they had frightened his mother.

He opened the side door of the bar, slowly, almost as if hoping to walk in unnoticed.

"Hey. Where were you yesterday? You go off because some kid throws orange juice all over your shirt, and then you don't come back. What's the matter? You frightened this kid is waiting to throw another one at you?"

Jamie was smiling, rubbing a broad yellow towel across the top of the wooden bar, preparing for the day. It would be cooler. A breeze was coming off the sea. He'd even heard someone suggest that rain was on the way. In July? Jamie had thought it unlikely.

"I'm sorry," said Joaquim, picking up a second towel and starting to wipe the small round tables, ordering the chairs that stood haphazardly around them. "It was my mother. She was ill."

"She better now?"

"Yes."

Sofia wasn't but she had insisted that Joaquim should go back to work. It was a good job and there were the costs of university looming round the corner. And then she had started crying again as she realized that it was a corner that they might not even reach.

"And that girl was in last night, looking for you."

Joaquim looked up.

"Denny?"

"With her uncle. They didn't stay long. Hey! Scram! *Xo! Xo!*"

126

Jamie flapped his towel at two large crows that had appeared at the edges of the bar, picking their way among the tables, ferreting with their beaks in the sand to prise out any scraps of food. Slowly they lifted into the air, beating their wings, one squawking in protest as it did so.

"Jamie."

"Yes?"

Jamie glanced across the bar. Joaquim's voice hadn't suggested that he was about to tell a joke.

"Do you know anything about the lobisomen?"

"The what?"

"The lobisomen."

Jamie smiled. Maybe there *was* a joke coming.

"You mean that old wives' tale about a female Dracula running round the place killing anything that moves and then taking over their bodies?"

Joaquim nodded.

"Something like that."

"No more than you do, I don't suppose. Only that they have a bonfire every year and everybody gets drunk. It's good for business."

Joaquim smiled briefly.

"You don't believe in it?"

Jamie stopped cleaning the bar, staring at Joaquim as if he had just turned into Santa Claus.

"Joaquim, are you serious?"

Joaquim pushed a steel-ribbed chair into place

under the table in front of him. One of its legs seemed to be slightly bent.

"No. Not really. But. . ."

"But?"

"Well, there are some people who do take it seriously."

"Tell me if you see one and I'll make sure I'm on the other side of the street."

"You've seen them yourself."

"I've seen them?"

Joaquim nodded, straightening for a moment.

"Yes. The *mordomos*. In the procession."

Jamie laughed.

"And the little man with the greasy hair dressed up as a nun?"

"The monk."

"Well, he's as mad as a hatter and as for the rest of them, they only do it because it lets them get away from their wives once in a blue moon and drink themselves under the table."

"My father's one."

"Now you're getting there."

For the first time Joaquim laughed and threw his towel across the bar, catching Jamie on the shoulder. As he did so, an elderly couple appeared by one of the tables, the woman carrying a wicker basket, her husband a folded copy of *The Times*. Neither looked in a very good mood.

Brushing the front of his shirt, Joaquim made his way through the tables towards them.

"Good morning. *Bon dia*. Can I help you?"

Jamie turned away, smiling. Like the prospect of rain, he thought it unlikely.

During the morning, the clouds had continued to build from the south. Low grey clouds moving in quickly from the sea.

Elliott watched them as he stood in the square, leaning against one of the tall, brightly-coloured, wooden posts that now stood like sentries round the Plaza Vilfeira. They were clouds he might have expected to see in November. Or December, when the charmless Algarvean winter shackled the coastline, bringing thick, early morning mists that clung to the earth and driving rain that scoured it.

The streets were busier this morning. Maybe the beaches held less appeal, given the threat of rain.

Elliott glanced at his watch. Quarter to twelve.

"I thought it didn't rain in the summer."

Elliott turned quickly. Denny was standing beside him.

"You finished?"

Denny nodded her head, holding up two bulging plastic bags.

"Something for everyone back home."

Elliott smiled.

"You'll need to buy another suitcase."

He held out his hands, offering to take the bags. Denny gave him one of them.

"We'll share."

They began to walk across the square. Already, the first drops of rain were in the wind, touching their faces and the bare skin of their arms. Denny glanced across at the tall pyramid of wood that now dominated the square's centre.

"I don't suppose they're going to be too pleased if it carries on raining for the next few days."

"Who?"

"The locals. I mean, I don't think wood burns too well when it's soaking wet."

Elliott laughed, briefly.

"The rain won't last. A summer storm, that's all. It'll be over by the end of the afternoon."

Denny stopped, gazing up at the towering pyre, trying to imagine it alight. And slowly into her mind, gathering shape and form like fish rising to the water's surface, there came the image of a woman. High cheekbones, long dark hair and deep black holes where her eyes had once been.

She turned away, grabbing Elliott by the arm, tightly. And started walking.

Jamie's Bar was almost empty. By now the rain was falling, a fine rain, driven across the wide, empty beaches by a wind that blew from the sea. Elliott sat at the bar, sipping a beer, talking to Jamie.

The elderly couple who had appeared earlier in the morning had moved to the shelter of the canopied roof that overhung the front of the bar and were now sitting in front of two cold cups of coffee, reading. Unsmiling.

Denny finished her Coke.

She left the small table where she had been sitting with Joaquim and walked out through the open door. It was warm. She felt the rain blowing against her face. Oddly, it felt welcome. Almost as if washing away the dust in the air, the heat of the morning and, with it, the face of the woman.

She began to walk out on to the beach, empty save for the upturned fishing boats, their bright colours now subdued by the low curtains of grey cloud that hung over them.

She felt the warm sand on the bare soles of her feet as she walked, each step silent, each one slow. And she thought of the last time the rain had been in her face. As they had carried Leyla from the cathedral and as, later, they had laid her coffin in the ground.

She stopped, bending down to the wet sand, picking it up in her hand, letting it run through her fingers. The soil she had dropped on the coffin lid had been dark. The Portuguese sand was light. The sand of the land to the west.

"I thought you might need company."

Denny turned, watching as Joaquim walked

through the sand towards her. He would be surprised to find her crying. She lifted her head, slowly.

"It was my fault."

Grey towers of Durham,
Yet well I love thy mixed and massive piles,
Half Church of God, half castle 'gainst the Scot,
And long to roam these venerable aisles,
With records stored of deeds long since forgot.

Leyla read the words out loud, half-smiling as she did so. And then looked up from the stone tablet that carried them, set into the warm, sandstone blocks of Prebends Bridge.

"What's a mixed and massive pile?"

"I don't know," said Denny. "But I expect it's poetry."

"Not much of a poem," said Leyla, turning again to the tablet, letting her gaze wander over Scott's words, written in 1820 to celebrate the writer's first sight of the cathedral. "But I liked the bit about the memories."

She turned back to Denny again.

"I'm afraid that we Irish are very fond of our memories."

Denny smiled.

"Come on. Let's go and find this ghost of yours."

The two girls left the poet's thoughts, etched into

the stone for the centuries that followed to share, and began to walk across the thin, medieval bridge, its three arches vaulting over the fast-flowing muddy swirl of the River Wear below.

It had been Leyla's idea. On holiday from her home in County Cork, staying with her friend and her family on the moors of Weardale, watching as the seemingly endless north-eastern English rain splashed across the windows, it had been her idea to go to the cathedral. To find the stone, to touch the grave, to see the ghost.

She'd found the story in the local paper. They ran it every year but it had been the first time Leyla had seen it. About the young woman from the eighteenth century who had been burnt as a witch and whose spirit was now said to haunt the vast, echoing chambers of the city's cathedral. That many years before, she had defied her father, then the cathedral's dean, and had run away to Europe with the man she had claimed to love. In time, the whispers had begun. That they had both died penniless on the streets of Paris. That she had been sold into slavery and that he had been hacked to death by Barbary pirates. Or, more bizarrely, that he had left her to join a monastery and had denounced her as a witch. Neither had ever returned to the city again.

Shortly before the dean died, a horse-drawn stagecoach had arrived in the cathedral grounds. In it, there had been a coffin. There had been nobody with the coffin. No messenger. No mourners. No explanation even, save for a handwritten letter that one of the two coach-drivers had given to the dean.

The dean was said to have read the letter, and then burnt it. Some days later there had been a short service in the cathedral's small Chapel of St Augustine. The records showed that no more than six people had attended. And, later, it had been the same six people who had stood round a small grave in the private cathedral churchyard, watching as the coffin had been lowered into the ground. It had not been heavy. Inside, there was only a small metal urn, holding the ashes of Elizabeth Pearson.

Her father, the dean, the very Reverend Brian Pearson, had died that very night and, in time, was buried beside his daughter. He died having spoken to no one about the contents of the letter.

"Elizabeth Pearson. Born April 18th, 1734. Died July, 1753, Portugal. Given by God. Taken by Man. In Spiritus."

Leyla looked up from the flat gravestone, its sharp, marbled edges softened by the stubby grass that grew around it.

"And she's the ghost?"

"So the story goes," said Denny.

"And she was a witch?"

"Nobody knows where that came from.

Nobody's even very sure if that's who's buried down there. It was the dean himself who filled in the ledger, saying it was his daughter. Maybe it was just wishful thinking. That she'd come back after all those years."

"What a sad little tale," said Leyla, kneeling now and stretching out her hands towards the cold, glistening marble of the gravestone.

"So, little Lizzie," she said gently, rubbing her fingers across the smooth, dark surface of the stone. "What happened to you?"

The world beyond the small graveyard had suddenly seemed to fall silent as Leyla slowly re-read the words of the stone, whispering them to herself, gazing deep into the blurred, reflected images of the leafless trees above.

"Given by God. Taken by Man. In Spiritus."

And, amongst the images, she did not, at first, see the woman.

The silhouette that was growing amongst the twisted, shuddering branches, the cowled figure that looked away and then, suddenly, the head that was turning, the pallor of the face that was slowly revealing itself beneath the cowl and the thin slit of the mouth that was now opening. And the holes where her eyes had been.

Leyla stood back, quickly, the cold spike of fear cutting through her body, her pulse suddenly hammering against her tightened skin, her eyes suddenly shut to the ugliness of what she had seen.

And then opened again, her head slowly turning back, inevitably, towards the stone. Lying silently in the grass, its dark, glistening surface still cold, still reflecting the slowly waving branches of the trees. Hiding the long-buried remains of the dean's daughter.

"I want to go."

The words were spoken quickly.

"What?" said Denny. "But we've. . ."

"I don't care," said Leyla. "I want to go. Now."

"But why. . .?"

"I saw something, that's all. Don't ask me, I don't know. . ."

"Hey. Come on."

Denny reached out for her friend, putting her arm around her shoulder. She was surprised to find that Leyla was shivering.

"Let's go and find a coffee."

It had once been the refectory. The dining-hall of the monks who had originally worshipped in the cathedral. A long, timber-roofed room, it was now a coffee shop, sharing the space with various stands and racks of souvenirs, books and paintings, each one, it seemed, inspired by the tall pillars and towers of the Norman building.

"The mixed and massive piles," said Denny.

Leyla smiled. She sipped her coffee, grateful for its warmth, comfortable again in the dusty, colourful, jumbled clutter of the shop where small children asked for ice-cream and mothers dutifully fingered through the coins in their purse. Sometimes. Leyla watched as a small boy began to cry as his mother continued to shake her head. The child wanted a small, golden teddy bear. His mother didn't. It seemed a curious toy to be selling in a cathedral.

"I think we should go up the tower."

Leyla looked back towards Denny.

"The what?"

"The tower. Now that we're here."

"But. . ."

Leyla lowered her cup, settling it in the small saucer on the wooden table. Denny was turning in her seat, reaching for her jacket.

"It's a terrific view."

"But it's raining."

Leyla's voice was quiet.

Denny seemed not to have noticed. She was standing now, smiling, encouraging her friend.

"No, it isn't. It's just damp. Come on."

"But, what if. . .?"

"What if what?"

"What if the woman. . .?"

"Leyla." Denny's voice hardened perceptibly, almost as if trying to shake her friend out of what was no more than a dream. "There is no woman. It's a story. No more. And if a ghost appeared every time anybody reads the words on a gravestone, then the world would be full of them."

"But Denny, it wasn't me she was looking at."

"I'm sorry?"

"She was looking past me, Denny. She was looking at you."

Denny pushed her chair back. And smiled.

"Then I'll look forward to meeting her. Now come on."

Leyla said nothing as she stood, taking her coat from the chair. Then smiled as she pushed the memory to the back of her mind. Denny was right. There was no woman.

Only a child that cried for a teddy bear and a mother that said no.

Denny saw her first.

Walking towards them as they crossed the broad, marble floor of the cathedral nave. Walking down the central aisle, the long wooden benches at either side empty, the congregation of Sunday now no more than ghosts.

Denny stopped. Half-turning, she felt Leyla take her arm, holding it, gripping it. Neither moved. Both watched in silence as the woman came towards them. Slowly. Her head bowed beneath a broad dark shawl, her footsteps echoing through the vaulting arches of fluted stone that bent across the shadowed depths of the building. She seemed small, her shoulders hunched, as if protecting her body from the chill of the afternoon.

Denny glanced away, looking for escape, her eyes moving quickly across the tall, thick pillars of stone. The dark wooden stalls of the choir. The narrow door, where a single bulb burned beneath the flags of regiments whose soldiers had died in pain on the battlefields of the world.

There was no woman. She knew that. And yet, her heart was now beating hard. Her fingers had stiffened. She could feel Leyla's grip tightening.

"Denny!"

Leyla's voice was harsh, frightened.

"Denny, she's. . ."

Denny turned back. Quickly. The footsteps had stopped. The woman was standing in front of them, her head lifting, her eyes meeting theirs, her mouth opening as she smiled.

"I wonder if you could tell me where I can get a cup of coffee?"

The silver cross that hung from her neck gleamed as it caught the distant light from the candles that burnt at the altar. And the nun instinctively reached for it as the two girls in front of her now started to laugh. Leaning on one another's shoulders, momentarily helpless, their laughter a desperate expression of profound relief – the creature from Hell no more than a nun with blue eyes, looking for a cup of coffee.

"Oh dear, was it something. . .?"

"No, no. . ." said Denny, wiping her hand across her eyes, stifling her laughter. "No. I'm sorry, forgive us."

Leyla straightened again, wiping the front of her coat as if brushing away the tears.

"What she means, Sister, is that we're very rude. And that you'd never believe us even if we told you."

"It's just that. . ." said Denny, smiling.

"It's just that nothing," said Leyla, interrupting her friend and taking the nun by the arm. "Now, just come with me. And I'll take you to the coffee."

The nun looked at Leyla, a broad smile on her face.

"County Cork?"

"Kinsale itself."

"A lovely town," said the nun, still smiling as she walked back down the aisle with the two girls. "They say God laid the bricks when they built Kinsale."

"But I don't understand," said Joaquim, as they walked slowly along the edges of the bay, each rippling wave streaming salt water across their feet as it ran over them and then drained into the soft, brown sand.

"What don't you understand?" said Denny, her face held up against the fine curtain of rain that still swept across the beach.

The distant headlands, their outline normally so clear against the deep blue skies of summer, now lay shrouded in a thick white mist that curled across their summit before falling slowly down their sides.

"OK, maybe you both got scared but I can't see that it was anyone's fault."

"I took her to the tower," said Denny, slowly, her mind drifting back to the grey colours of that April afternoon.

"Yes," said Joaquim. "And you ran into a ghost. Only it wasn't a ghost. It was a nun. And you took her for coffee."

"You're right," said Denny. "You don't understand."

She stopped, turning her head towards Joaquim, her long dark hair hanging wet about the sides of her face and trailing over the brown skin of her shoulders.

"And you don't understand because I haven't told you."

Joaquim stood, watching her, seeing the unhappiness in her eyes.

"What haven't you told me?"

Denny looked past him, her gaze wandering across the wide grey body of the sea, shifting uneasily beneath the ceaseless rain.

"That we went back to the tower. That Leyla had already tried to warn me. And I ignored her. Laughed at her."

Denny's voice was quiet. Lonely.

"And that. . . That was my fault."

At the foot of the stairs, they had passed an elderly Japanese couple. The husband had smiled and said, in almost perfect English, that it was a very long climb to the top and that his wife was exhausted. But that the view had been worth it. Looking at the strained, damp face of his wife and the heaving movement of her chest, neither Denny nor Leyla were entirely sure that she would have agreed with him.

The stairs were broad at first, almost welcoming. As if to persuade the newcomer that the climb would not be too difficult after all. They were built in flights of eighteen steps, each flight taking its visitor gradually upwards before finally turning back upon itself and offering a further eighteen, imperceptibly steeper and climbing always towards the galleries above. From there, a thinner, circular stone staircase led to the summit of the tower itself.

Denny had climbed the stairs many times. She led the way, Leyla climbing more slowly, catching glimpses of the world outside through the slits that had been originally cut into the thick stone walls of the staircase to provide a source of light. In more recent years electric light had been added, even if that meant little more than a bare lightbulb at occasional intervals, hanging from the low ceiling, glowing feebly.

"Come on," said Denny, turning to look for her friend.

"I hope it's worth it," said Leyla, beginning now, after almost twenty minutes, to feel the pain of the climb.

"If that Japanese lady could—"

"I know," said Leyla. "I know."

The galleries were just over four hundred feet above the ground. Originally, this had been the height of the tower. The remaining two hundred feet had been added at the behest of an over-zealous bishop of the twelfth century who had argued that the extra height meant that the cathedral would be closer to God.

"And they believed him?" said Leyla.

"Some folk will in believe anything," said Denny, smiling.

Leyla laughed, her deep blue eyes sparkling once again.

"Don't tell me. Even in strange women crawling out of graves."

They were now standing at the edge of the galleries.

Through the open door ahead of them, they could see the thin walkway that ran round the four walls of the tower. From here, the visitor could look down to the patterned marble floor of the nave far below.

"That's it over there," said Denny.

"What?"

Denny was pointing to a small door set into the far wall.

"The staircase to the roof."

"We've got to walk round the walls?"

"It's easy," said Denny. "Just don't look down."

She stepped out on to the walkway. It was narrow, the walls of the tower on one side, a low, stone rail running along the other. Leyla waited, watching her friend move forwards, knowing that she had to follow. She stepped out carefully. Then stopped. There had been the sound of a footstep on the stairs behind. Perhaps she would wait. Perhaps whoever it was would walk round with her, since Denny was now already halfway along the wall. It would be easier with someone beside her.

She looked back, staring through the open door and into the shadows of the staircase behind her. There was no movement. No sound. She waited. Denny was now almost at the end of the wall. And was turning, waving at her friend.

"Come on!"

The whisper echoed through the open space of the tower.

Leyla looked back to the stairs again. Still

silence. She turned away and began to edge slowly along the walkway, her gaze firmly on Denny. She sensed the open space at her side but brought her mind to think only of the wall beside her. The thick, stone wall of the cathedral tower.

And then she heard the breathing. And smelt the acrid, pungent smell of the breath. And felt the presence of the creature behind her. Wide-eyed, she turned quickly. And felt the cold hands suddenly fasten on to her neck. She screamed, lashing out at the creature with her fists, terrified by the manic shrieking and in sudden, hideous pain as the fingernails began to rip at the flesh of her throat.

"Run, Denny! Run!"

"Leyla!"

Denny screamed out Leyla's name, unable to move, or to think, frozen against the stone tower wall. All that she could see was the body of her friend, now bent back against the stone rail, her hands clutching at her neck, her legs kicking as if she had suddenly been gripped by some powerful and yet invisible attacker. And the blood running down the sides of her neck. And, as Denny began to run back towards her, she had seen her friend falling backwards over the low stone rail, her body spinning slowly down towards the cold marble of the floor far below.

She had plunged into the stone and there had

been silence. And, as Denny had stared from the tower above, it seemed to her that a figure had moved from the broken body of her friend and disappeared into the cold, unforgiving shadows of the cathedral, Moving quickly at the sudden approach of the nun.

"And you think she was killed by a ghost?"

"I don't know." Denny was crying, letting the tears run slowly down her cheeks, only to be washed away by the rain. "I didn't see anything. But she seemed to be fighting someone. Or something. She was screaming at me to run away. Almost as if she was protecting me."

"And then she fell?"

"Yes."

Denny looked at Joaquim, as if looking for absolution.

"I ignored her. She said she'd seen a woman. She was frightened. We should have gone home."

Joaquim held out his hand.

"Denny, there was no woman. No ghost. Your friend fell."

And, as they walked slowly back along the beach towards the small bar, so the rain began to ease.

11

It was hot.

The rains of the day before had cleared away to the east and, once again, the sun burnt the dusty fields and cottages of the Algarve as it climbed into the morning sky.

Joao straightened his back, wiping his brow in the welcome shade of the thick, cork oak tree. The trees grew along the sides of a low hill that rose from the level of the plain and from here, Joao could turn and let his gaze sweep over the distant roofs of Vilfeira, the beaches beyond and the curl of the bay as it ran away from him towards the east.

"You told your wife."

The voice was soft. The menace it contained unmistakable. Joao paused and then turned, quickly.

The monk was standing at the side of the dirt track that twisted its way through the cork trees. In his hands, he carried a thick wooden stick. His feet were bare.

"I. . ."

Joao's voice faltered. The eyes of the monk, like those of the snake, seemed unblinking.

"Why?"

"I didn't—"

"Don't lie to me, you miserable pig!"

"She heard us. Talking."

Joao spoke quickly, almost as if to rid himself of the words of confession.

"Emilio. Emilio and I were talking. Quietly. Late at night. I didn't think that anyone could—"

"How much does she know?"

Joao shook his head.

"She won't say anything."

"How much?"

Joao let his head drop.

"I don't know."

"Does she know about the girl?"

Joao nodded.

In the branches above them, a small tree sparrow chipped at the oak bark with its short stubby beak, winkling out the insects that lived in the skin of the tree. Joao lifted his head again.

"She won't talk."

The monk's face remained expressionless. He

moved the stick from one hand to the other. And then nodded slowly, his eyes still fastened on the sweating face of the man in front of him.

"Perhaps we should make sure of that."

He pointed to the ground.

"Kneel."

Elliott stirred his coffee slowly, watching as the movement of the spoon spread ripples across the surface of the liquid. Satisfied, after some moments, that the sugar had dissolved, he lifted the spoon out, laid it in the saucer and, picking up the cup in his fingers, began to drink, carefully. The coffee was hot. Inside the villa, the phone rang, its harsh, demanding tones echoing across the stone floors of the rooms. Upstairs, he heard Denny answer it, her voice happy, her words indistinct. He took another sip of coffee, standing at the edge of the lawn, watching as Emilio walked across the gardens towards him. The gardener walked slowly, almost as if reluctant to meet Elliott.

"Boa tarde, Emilio!"

Elliott raised his hand in the air, smiling. Emilio waved back, briefly, without speaking.

By the time he reached Elliott, thin lines of sweat were beginning break down the sides of his face. He was breathing deeply. And Elliott picked up the familiar smell. *Medronho*. He knew that Emilio rarely started the morning without it.

149

"Señor."

Emilio's voice seemed distant, as if it had not been his. The voice, rather, of the ventriloquist lending his words to a stuffed rag doll, distorted, strained. He spoke in Portuguese.

Upstairs, Denny had heard the two men. She opened her bedroom windows, walking out on to the warm, dark red tiles of the balcony. She leant on the thin metal railings that ran round it, looking out over the pool and gardens below.

Emilio looked up. He seemed almost surprised to see her. Denny didn't wave. Or call out. And the gardener looked away again, quickly, almost furtively. As if afraid to be seen or heard. Denny wondered how many lizards he had butchered that morning.

Elliott was nodding, finishing his coffee. Then he turned and walked back towards the villa, leaving Emilio to stand watching him for some moments before glancing up towards Denny again and then turning to walk away.

Denny heard Elliott walk into the villa, crossing the stone floor of the hallway below.

"Denny!"

His voice rang up the stairs. Denny left the balcony, walking back through the bedroom, stopping at the head of the curling staircase. Elliott was looking up at her.

"I'm going into Vilfeira. Emilio's just told

me he's seen Mateus. The shutters are ready. You coming?"

Denny paused for a moment, then shook her head.

"It's too hot."

"You don't want to see Joaquim?"

"He's working." Denny smiled. "But that was him on the phone. We've been invited to his home this evening."

"Joaquim's?"

"His mum's cooking. And apparently, they're celebrating."

"Celebrating what?"

"I don't know. Something to do with his father."

Elliott laughed.

"OK, I'll get some wine. And you're sure you don't want to come?"

Denny shook her head again, turning away from the stairs.

"No. This morning's a sitting-by-the-pool morning. And don't worry about me. . ." She looked back down the stairs at her uncle. "Lucilia's going to be here soon. And there's always the lizard-killer wandering around outside."

Elliott nodded and, waving a brief goodbye, walked across the room towards the front door, leaving the empty coffee cup on the broad, glass dining-table as he passed it.

"Bye."

Denny's voice followed him as he left the house, closing the door softly behind him. He walked across the short driveway towards the jeep, aware suddenly that Emilio was watching him. He said nothing. He climbed into the jeep, kicked its engine into life and pushed the gears into reverse.

Moments later, he was on the road, spinning the wheel, turning towards Vilfeira. Looking back briefly, he saw Denny waving from the upstairs balcony, a blue swimming-towel over her shoulder. He waved back. And then saw Emilio stoop towards a pile of sticks by the shed. He pulled something out of his pocket. Matches. And then struck one, holding it to the dried wood, watching as the fire flickered into life.

As Elliott began to drive slowly away from the villa, he could see the thin trail of light blue smoke begin to drift upwards into the morning skies. It seemed odd. No one lit fires during the long, hot, dog days of the Algarvean summer.

"Joaquim! Joaquim!"

Joaquim turned in the faded leather seat as his mother ran from the small, roadside cottage, waving her arms, shouting to make herself heard above the rumble of her son's bike. He eased the throttle back, braking, throwing up a fine curtain of dust as the thick rubber tyres dragged across the edges of the road.

"You forgot!"

The bike stopped. Joaquim wiped the back of his hand across his forehead, the pores of his skin thick with sweat in the heat of midday.

His mother slowed to a walk, reaching into the deep folds of her long, brightly patterned dress, pulling out a tightly wrapped, white paper parcel.

"You said. . ."

"I know," said Joaquim, as Sofia now stopped beside him.

"And it won't take you long."

"But Mama, I'm already late. Jamie. . ."

Sofia pushed the parcel into Joaquim's hands. He nodded, smiling. Without his cheese and bread, his father's day would be a very long one.

"And you did ask your friends, yes?"

Joaquim nodded.

"I spoke to Denny a few minutes ago."

"Good. Then tonight, we celebrate."

She smiled.

Joaquim leant forward, kissing her lightly on the cheek. It was the first time he'd seen her smile for days. He studied her face closely, looking for the flickers in her eyes or the tremble of her muscles that would tell him that she had lied. But there were none. His mother's dark eyes looked steadily back at her son. She had told Joaquim the truth.

That, the night before, Joao had said the monk was mad and that he, Joao, would have no more to do with the procession. That the monk could carry the cage himself. That Manuel had disappeared, almost certainly, to the bars of Playa Crienca, further down the coast. Everyone knew that's where he always went to get drunk after his wife threw him out. Which she did. Often. And as far as Emilio was concerned: if Joao left, then, for sure, Emilio would follow.

That it was all lunacy, anyway. Sofia was right. The man was mad. In fact, he probably wasn't even a monk. Just an old tramp, telling stories and barking at the moon.

And, that they had then gone to bed, Sofia no longer crying, content at last that her husband had freed himself of the nightmares he had conjured up, talking with Emilio in the small hours of the night. Perhaps that was all it had been. A nightmare. A dream.

And, as Joao had lain in bed that night beside his wife, he had listened to the cicadas of the countryside, beyond the sleeping village, spinning their chattering, musical web across the dark shadows of the fields and twisted cork trees. He had listened. But had not seen the shadow of the bird drifting slowly across the skies.

The shadow of the sequoia.

"And are you sure he meant it?"

Joaquim heard himself asking the question again

154

as the wheels of the bike felt their way along the corrugated, dried mud of the twisting goat-track. And, once again, he could see his mother's face, her eyes bright, her smile honest. She had known that Joao had meant it. That it had all been very foolish and they would all feel very embarrassed, if ever the truth were to be told. Joaquim smiled as he now, at last, saw the oak trees.

Late already for Jamie's Bar, he'd taken a short cut across the open countryside, avoiding the road. And had lost himself among the dry, anonymous fields and tall grasses that stretched across the plains.

Still several hundred metres away, he could not see his father as he approached the trees. It had to be this plantation. It was the only one near the village where the bark would be cut this year. As he rode the bike across the open land, he glanced down again to make sure that his father's lunch was still hanging from the seat, the fragile paper parcel held there by a length of string.

He looked up again. There was no movement beneath the trees, where the few shadows that had escaped from the pitiless gaze of the midday sun overhead now seemed to cower beneath the thick, tangled branches. Joao would be there, leaning against a tree trunk, the smoke from his cigarette curling into the leaves, his limbs without movement in the heat of the day.

And then Joaquim saw the bodies. Lying at the side of the road. Both quite still. The blood from his father's head now drying in the dirt around him. The twisted, hideously angled body beside him a silent witness to the death of a man who had died in agony, clutching at his stomach.

Joaquim dropped the bike and ran, shouting, across the field, finally reaching the two men, standing above them, staring at the hideous wound on the side of Joao's head. And the holes in Manuel's face and neck left by the teeth of the snake.

It was Thursday. Two days until the festival. *Fogo de Arteficio*. As Elliott drove through the sunburnt streets of Vilfeira, he could feel the atmosphere beginning to kindle in the life of the pavements and shops. The posters. The coloured streamers that had begun to loop and curl downwards from what seemed to be every upstairs window in the town. The almost seamless bursts of music that sprayed from opened doors and windows.

Elliott had avoided the festival since Isobel's death but, as he wound the open-topped jeep through the narrow streets, slowly the sense of expectancy began to feed into him. Above him, draped from one side of the street to the other, a broad yellow banner boasted that there was "Something in the Air".

"Algo para Acontecer."

Elliott smiled. Many years before, it had been a song. An anthem of revolution, paraded by a band with the unlikely name of Thunderclap Newman. Perhaps the designer of the poster had also known the song.

Elliott realized that his route through the town was taking him very much along the same streets that the procession would use. Through the old quarter, the houses that had survived the earthquakes. Past the statue of Vasco Da Gama, who, so legend had it, had been born near the town. Along the cobbles of the Rua del Morte. Past the small church of Sao Clemente, where the priest would add his blessing to the *mordomos* and their charge. And finally into the Rua da Galacia, the broad street that led to the town square, where the tall pyramid of wood waited for its victim.

Elliott drove on through the square, taking the Rua Casa do Ouro, the road that led up towards the headlands behind the town, where once there had indeed been a house whose walls had been inlaid with tiny flecks of gold leaf, so that, when the sun fell upon it, it had glowed as if entirely made of gold. The house had collapsed with the earthquakes and now, over two hundred years later, the stumps of its walls, barely visible above the folds of the hard, baked earth, were all that remained of its former glory.

Elliott pulled off the road and into the small workshop yard that stood facing the ruins of the golden house. He turned the engine off, letting its grumbling notes fade into the morning air. And then sat, waiting.

There was little point in going to look for Mateus. When the old carpenter was ready, he would appear. Elliott could hear the sawing of wood, coming from the small shed at the back of the yard. Apparently, Mateus was not ready.

Elliott wished he had remembered to tell Denny about Lucilia. As he sat, his head leaning back against the seat, his face taking in the warmth of the sun, he could hear her saying that she would be there soon.

She wouldn't. She was ill. That was what Emilio had also told him.

"Ah, Señor. Boa tarde."

Elliott opened his eyes, pulling himself up in the seat, turning towards the voice.

The old man was walking slowly across the yard towards the jeep, a broad smile on his face, his faded blue overalls hanging loosely from his shoulders and flapping at his heels. As he neared the jeep, he held out a thin, wiry hand.

"Señor Elliott."

Elliott laughed and climbed out of the jeep, taking the old man's hand.

"Mateus. Todo bem?"

158

"OK," said the carpenter. "Apparently *he* doesn't want to see me just yet."

And he pointed upwards towards the sky, grinning.

"And not for many years, I'm sure," said Elliott.

Mateus waved his hand back towards the shed.

"Some coffee, perhaps?"

"Sounds good," said Elliott.

"And I know why you've come," said the carpenter, as they walked slowly across the yard. "And I'm sorry but, you know, it's old age. I get slower. And you musn't be cross with an old man."

Elliott laughed.

"Cross?"

"Yes, just because I haven't finished your shutters, so you come up here to be cross. I know you English. But you wait till you taste my coffee. *E magnifica*. It takes away. . . Señor?"

Elliott had stopped walking.

"But, Mateus, I thought they were ready. I mean, it's not a problem but. . ."

The carpenter frowned, slight puzzlement in his eyes as he looked now at Elliott.

"But why did you think they were ready? Another day. Maybe two. But not yet."

"But Emilio said. . ."

"Emilio?" The carpenter's eyes narrowed. "What did Emilio say?"

Elliott shrugged his shoulders, aware of the

unease that had crept into the sunlight of the morning.

"That he'd met you this morning, That you'd told him the shutters were ready. That I could pick them up."

"Señor. . ."

The old man paused for a moment, not quite sure of what was happening or of what was being said.

"Señor, I haven't seen Emilio this morning."

The water was brackish. The rain of the day before had done little more than stir the waters of the small pool, churning up the mud beneath the surface, breaking up the thick green film of slime that covered it.

But it was water.

Holding it in cupped hands, Joaquim opened his fingers slowly, letting the liquid fall gently on to the side of his father's head.

There was nothing he could do for Manuel. The man's body was stiff, his skin cold. Cold, even beneath the pitiless glare of the sun. But Joao had been breathing. Faintly at first, stronger now as the cold water splashed on to his skin, soaking in to the nerve-ends, waking the dulled corners of his brain.

His eyes flickered.

"Papa!"

Joaquim's voice was quiet, urgent. As if afraid he might be overheard. He moved quickly back to the pool, cupping more water in his hands and letting it fall on to the wound. The dried blood, now moistened, began to wash away, soaking into the rough cloth of Joao's shirt.

Joao's eyes were now open. Staring hard across the rough dirt of the road. His sight was blurred. Shadows crept in front of him. Somewhere, someone was saying something. The same word, over and over.

"Papa."

Joaquim now took his father's head in his hands, wiping the wound gently with the cuffs of his shirt. Joao's eyes turned towards him, staying with him, trying to clear the blurred outline that knelt over him.

"Joaquim, I. . ."

"Don't speak, Papa. Be still."

The shepherd had seen them as he followed his drifting, straggling flock of sheep across the fields towards the cork trees. At first, he had thought they might have been cork-cutters, taking time out for lunch at the side of the road. But, as he drew nearer, he saw the pain on the dead man's face. And the wound at the side of the second man's head, the blood on his shirt. And the boy, holding his right arm, helping the man to his feet.

The shepherd ran forwards, dropping the cloth bag that had been looped over his shoulder.

"Let me help."

He took Joao's other arm, supporting him, holding firm as they now began to take Joao's weight. Joao could hear the sheep but could see no more than their shadows moving at the edges of his vision.

"Thank you," he said slowly, his voice hoarse. "And you, Joaquim, my son," he added, letting his head fall against Joaquim's shoulder. *"Obrigado."*

And then he spoke slowly, quietly.

"Joaquim."

"Yes, Papa."

"Can you see the bay?"

Joaquim nodded.

"Yes."

"And the houses by the sand?"

"Yes."

Joao paused, as if unwilling to ask the last question. And then he spoke.

"And tell me, do you see the smoke of a fire?"

Joaquim's eyes narrowed, closing on the villas hidden in amongst the pinewoods at the edge of the sea. Elliott's was there. Somewhere. At first, he saw nothing and then, drifting through the trees and into the air above them, Joaquim saw the blue smoke of a fire. Smoke that spiralled slowly upwards, melting into the skies beneath the shadows of the sequoia, circling high above.

"Yes, Papa. There is a fire."

Carefully, Joao turned his head towards his son, his eyes half-seeing, their tears glistening in the brilliant glare of the sunlight.

"Joaquim. . ."

His voice was low. Halting. Frightened.

"Joaquim, I am so sorry."

And the shepherd, who now knew who these men were, knew he was telling the truth.

"Denny!"

Elliott had thrown the front door open, ignoring the sound as its metal handle hammered into the white plaster of the walls.

"Denny!"

He ran to the stairs, throwing himself up them, the pulse at the side of his head beating hard, his hands damp with sweat. The bathroom was empty. So was Denny's bedroom, where the wind blew gently through the open windows. From the balcony he stared anxiously over the gardens, the pool, the lawn where no more than an hour before, he had spoken to Emilio.

"Denny!"

Each time he shouted, so his voice became more desperate, more frightened.

The villa was empty. The pool deserted. A blue

towel was draped over one of the wooden chairs at its side. A half-opened book lay on the table, its pages fanned open by the breeze. An empty glass stood beside it.

He stood still, his heart pumping hard, hoping to hear Denny's voice. Or the sound of her footsteps on the stone floors of the villa. Or to see her walk from the gardens, a small lizard in her hands. But nothing moved. Save for the small birds in the pines. And the last traces of smoke from the fire.

12

The bar was busy, alive to the sound of voices, the laughter of children, the clatter of metal knives and forks and the shrieks of gulls, fighting in the sand for the scraps of food thrown to them from the tables.

"No, I haven't seen either of them," said Jamie, squeezing the metal top off a green bottle and pouring the cold lager into a glass.

"Was he supposed to have been here today?" said Elliott.

"Yes," said Jamie, smiling. "But this is Portugal."

He bent down, reaching under the broad, polished wood of the counter, looking for a second bottle.

"You want a beer?"

Elliott shook his head.

"No. But thanks, anyway. I think. . . Jamie, have you any idea where. . .?"

Jamie shrugged his shoulders.

"You could try his house."

Elliott nodded. He knew the village.

"OK. Catch up with you later."

"You do that."

Jamie lifted his glass. And then smiled as Elliott turned and began to cross the bar.

"Hey, Elliott."

Elliott stopped, looking back towards the barman.

"Just don't worry, that's all. They're OK. Just kids being kids." Elliott nodded slowly.

"Sure."

As he drove, Elliott ran the morning through his head, almost unaware of the crazy lurching of the jeep as he threw it along the rutted, dried country roads.

Emilio had lied. It meant nothing. The man was probably drunk. The gardener rarely smelt of anything but *medronho*. And the villa, empty, the doors unlocked, the windows open? Joaquim must have appeared out of the blue. Suggested a drive somewhere. Breakfast. Lunch. A gallon of *medronho*. Any damn thing.

The jeep slewed violently across the dirt as Elliott swerved to avoid an animal crawling out of the ditch at the side of the road. A sheep. A goat. He didn't know. Didn't care. He pushed the vehicle harder, listening to the engine howl as it ground its way up the slope towards the village. The slope, where, less than a week before, Joaquim had asked his father for the truth. And had been told the truth was nonsense.

The village was quiet. The jeep moved slowly down the main street, Elliott looking closely at the small, white cottages that ran at its sides. The tangled gardens that surrounded them. The faded, torn posters that hung limply from their walls, their colours long bleached by the sun, the bull-fights they once advertised long since won and lost, the blood of the bulls swept up with the sand, the broken bones of the *toureiros* now once more fused together.

Elliott knew vaguely what Joaquim's mother looked like. He'd seen her once or twice in Jamie's bar, watching almost proudly as her son moved from table to table, smiling, laughing. Growing slowly into a man. And now she stood by the front door of her small cottage, watching as the jeep grew closer. It was almost as if she had been expecting Elliott.

"Boa tarde, Señor."

The jeep's engine seemed to rattle briefly as Elliott switched it off, letting the dust in the air behind him settle, pulling himself out of the seat.

"Boa tarde, Señora," he said, walking behind the jeep, joining her beside the door. He knew she was alone. That it might yet be that her son Joaquim and Denny were both safe. That even now, they might be walking through the villa's front door. But he knew they were not here.

"Can I help?"

Elliott smiled, briefly.

"I'm sorry. My name's Hardy. Elliott Hardy. And you're. . .?"

Sofia held out her hand.

"Sofia. Joaquim's mother. But I think you may be a little early."

"Early?"

"Joaquim said he phoned this morning. I hope you can both come."

Elliott's mind blurred and then, almost as quickly, the pieces began to fall into place. Denny's voice. The morning phone call. Would they have supper with Joaquim's family? This evening.

He laughed. It seemed so long ago. He turned back.

"Señora, I. . ."

He wondered for a moment how to tell Sofia that her son was missing. That Denny was missing. He didn't.

"Señora, your son, Joaquim. Do you know where he is?"

He waited for her to say no. Or even, at Jamie's Bar. The proof that something had gone wrong. But she smiled, turning towards the fields beyond the village, pointing towards the dark shadows of the cork trees that fringed the lower slopes of the hills.

"He took Joao his cheese and bread. Half an hour ago. I don't know. Maybe longer."

The smile faded.

"Is he in trouble? Tell Jamie it's my fault. I asked him. . ."

"No, no. . ." Elliott shook his head. "There's no trouble. It's just that I. . ."

He paused, letting the fears slowly sharpen in his mind.

"Señora, was Denny with him?"

Sofia shook her head.

"Not when he left. But then, I don't know. Maybe he picked her up."

She looked at Elliott, seeing the worry gathering in his eyes.

"Try that road."

She pointed to the small track that turned off the main village street by the Café Julia.

"Thank you."

Elliott had turned and was now walking back round the jeep, running the fingers of his hand through his thick, greying hair. As he climbed back behind the wheel, flicking the ignition switch, letting the engine bark into life, he remembered Lucilia. Joaquim's aunt.

"And send my best wishes to your sister. I hope she's better soon."

"Lucilia?"

"Emilio told me she was ill."

He swung the wheel, glancing back over his shoulder, letting the jeep move out into the road. He turned back briefly as he now began to pull away from the cottage, waving.

"See you this evening."

Sofia lifted her hand, her lips saying goodbye but her voice silent. She had seen Lucilia earlier in the morning. Not long after Emilio had told her sister not to go up to Elliott's house today. Elliott, he had said, was having guests.

He could see them in the distance. Their outlines blurred by the heat rising from the ground, moving slowly along the edge of the track. Briefly, Elliott wondered why Joaquim wasn't on his bike. And then realized. It had broken down. That's why nobody had seen them. That's why they were late.

There were three of them. One seemed to be leaning on another's shoulder. At this distance, he couldn't see who it was. He hoped it wasn't Denny.

He tried to push the jeep faster across the jagged, broken road surface but, as the wheels hammered against the raw, uneven edges of the pot-holes, so the vehicle's frame juddered as if to break in half.

Elliott swore. Sweating heavily as the sun burnt the skin of his shoulders, impatient as he closed on the blurred figures ahead.

Three men.

Elliott braked, screwing the dust from the road, sending it swirling above his head as the tyres bit into the earth. He cut the power, letting the silence of the countryside close once again over the scar of the jeep's howling engine. The distant call of small birds. The soft wind blowing through the tall, dried grasses. The smell of woodsmoke in the air.

He recognized Joaquim. The man leaning on his shoulder, he guessed, must be his father, Joao. The third man he didn't know. He climbed out of the jeep as they moved slowly closer, almost shuffling along the edge of the track. Elliott began to walk towards them, his eyes searching the countryside for signs of Denny. Or of what had happened.

Joao was hurt. Elliott could see the scar on the side of his head, the blood that had dried along its line, and on his clothes.

"Joaquim."

He spoke quietly as he neared the three men. As if at a hospital bedside.

Joaquim had seen the jeep when it had ben no more than a trace of dust threading its way through

the uneven, bare fields. He'd known it was Elliott.
And Denny. He was surprised to find Elliott alone.

"Señor?"

Elliott looked at Joao.

"Your father?"

Joaquim nodded.

"What happened?"

"Nothing." Joao's voice was low, hoarse.
Through half-closed, reddened eyes, he looked
carefully at Elliott. "Nothing happened."

"But. . ."

"I fell. Nothing else. *Nada*."

Elliott let his eyes drift across towards the third
man. The shepherd, a thick wooden staff in one
hand, a cloth bag thrown over his shoulder.

"There is another one."

The man spoke slowly.

"Another?"

"By the side of the road. He's dead."

Elliott looked back towards Joaquim.

"He was called Manuel," said Joaquim.

"A *mordomo*."

Joao's voice was faint, his mind drifting back to
the sight of his friend in the dust, his hands
clutching his stomach, his face stiff with pain.

"I thought you said that nothing happened. . ."

Elliott looked at Joao. And paused. The man's
eyes had closed. "I think we should get him home."

Joaquim nodded, moving his father's limp body

towards the jeep, easing him into the passenger seat, closing the metal door slowly.

Elliott found himself looking at the shepherd, standing quite still, his hands clasped across the roughly-carved head of the stick on which he leant.

"You know what happened. Don't you?"

The shepherd shrugged his shoulders, slowly, his face shaded by the peak of his dark blue cap.

"I know it was the monk."

"Denny is missing?"

Joaquim said the words slowly, almost absent-mindedly. As if he didn't understand them. As if Elliott had suddenly gone mad.

They stood in the road outside the cottage, their eyes narrowed against the glare of the early afternoon sun. Through the open door behind them, they could hear the sound of splashing water rattling against the tin sides of the small washroom basin as Sofia cleaned her husband's wound.

Elliott leant back against the side of the jeep, flinching slightly as the hot metal burnt through the thin cloth of his shirt.

"There was no note. Nothing. I assumed she'd gone somewhere with you."

Joaquim said nothing, his mind drifting back to his father's words of the night before. That it had all been nonsense. That the monk was mad. Not even a monk. A tramp, barking at the moon. And that the girl would be safe.

Suddenly, Joaquim turned, moving quickly towards the door, disappearing into the shadows beyond it. Elliott didn't follow. Joao's head was bowed over the small basin, his eyes closed as Sofia rubbed the side of his face with a towel.

"Where the hell is she?"

Joaquim's voice was loud, harsh, echoing through the cold, white rooms. Joao started, his head jerking upwards, surprised by the anger in his son's voice. He twisted towards him, standing upright, the pain from the wound cycling through the soft tissues of his brain. He said nothing. Watching only as the boy now moved towards him, his eyes bright, his gaze held on his father.

"Denny."

Joaquim was whispering now, the small washroom suddenly a confessional, the silence that of a church.

"Where is she?"

They walked throughout the afternoon.

Crossing the dried fields, threading their way through the occasional thin groups of tall cypress trees, staying close to what cover the plains offered. Emilio led them, having long given up waiting for Joao. He assumed something must have happened to him. It was impossible that he had not seen the smoke.

His eyes scanned the hills as, slowly, they drew closer. Parts now lay in shadow as the late afternoon sun began to fall through the skies, towards the west. The ruins were indistinct. It would be another hour before they reached them.

"And you want me to believe all this rubbish?"

The captain lit a cigarette, the small flame of the match flickering briefly in the gloom of the *esquadra da policia*.

"No," said Elliott, slowly. "I don't want you to believe it. I don't want to believe it. But I do want you to consider it as a possibility."

"As a what?"

"A possibility."

"Don't be ridiculous."

"It's worth a try."

"It's worth nothing!" The police captain hammered his fist into the desk. "And let me tell you that the only danger she's ever likely to find herself in is being fleeced by these local idiots and their seaside junk shops. Your daughter—"

"Niece."

"Whatever she is, right now, she's probably back in your villa, helping herself to a drink and doing what all these brats do on holiday. Nothing!"

"You could stop the procession."

The captain drew deeply on his cigarette, letting the smoke curl slowly out of the corners of his mouth.

"I could what?"

Elliott watched him carefully. He knew of the man's reputation.

"Stop the procession. If we can't find her, then you've got no choice."

The captain stood up, walking slowly round the desk, stopping in front of Elliott.

"I don't think you understand, my friend. I'm the only one that does have a choice. The procession goes ahead. That's my choice. And you've got exactly five seconds to stop wasting my time and get out of my sight." The captain smiled. "That's also my choice."

Elliott turned away, walking back towards the door. And then stopped, looking back.

"I don't understand."

"Understand what?"

"Why you won't help."

The policeman began to laugh. He stubbed his cigarette out in the small, patterned ashtray that sat on the desk. And then looked up.

"I won't help you because I don't believe you. Go home, Elliott. Go home and find your niece. Go home and leave the people of Vilfeira to their ways. God knows, there's little enough of the old world left."

"And if those ways include kidnapping?"

"And don't start all that nonsense again, *compinxa*. You're either drunk or you're a fool. Or maybe both. I don't know and I don't care. I just want you out of here."

"So you won't help."

"She'll turn up."

"And if she doesn't?"

"Then we'll all get on a magic carpet and go and look for her."

Elliott opened the door, looking back across the small, smoke-filled room.

"You don't believe a word I've said, do you?"

The policeman shook his head. He knew that every word of Elliott's wild story was true. But that it was a story whose ending had already been written. And, as Elliott left the room, the captain smiled, thinking of the monk and the promise he had made.

"The golden crosses of Santa Venezia. Yours."

For a badly paid, forgotten policeman in a backwater of the Algarve, for him, at least, the story's ending would be a happy one.

The long shadow thrown by the gibbet now reached back towards the small, stunted fir trees that clung to the side of the hills, their roots clutching at what little soil they could find. The sun, low in the sky, laced the plains and hills of the

Algarve with the warm, deep red glow of the evening, waking the cicadas and touching the feathers of the small birds drifting through the sky, seeking their roost for the night.

The monk watched them climb, their shadows long across the hillside. Six men. And the small donkey, its head bobbing slowly up and down as it moved up the hill.

"So, they've arrived."

The monk turned quickly, almost as if woken suddenly from sleep.

"Is it finished?"

The man standing behind him nodded, the thick veins on his neck pulsing hard against his skin. The monk now looked beyond the man, towards the trees, towards the tall, thick pole standing in the ground and the wooden beam that ran across its top. No wider than the spread of outstretched arms. High enough to let a body swing free above the ground. At each end of the beam hung a leather strap, moving slightly in the gentle evening wind that reached up from the plains below.

Four men stood beneath it. They had worked through the long hours of the afternoon, carrying the wood from the caves, breaking up the ground, cracking the rock, somehow jamming the frame of the gibbet into the unyielding stone of the hills.

The monk watched the trails of sweat curling down the man's face. Looking into his eyes, he could see the fear. The fear he had seen when he had first spoken to them. When they had seen the face in the waters of the well. When they had learnt what must be done.

"There is no other way."

The man nodded. But said nothing.

"He wouldn't listen!"

Elliott slammed the door behind him. The noise echoed across the stone floors and walls of the villa.

Joaquim left the patio, pulling open the tall French windows, watching as Elliott moved quickly across the room.

"You haven't found her?"

"What chance have I got when even the police don't want to know? Do you know what he said? Do you know what that damn fool in his grubby uniform called me? A waste of time. A waste of his lousy, meaningless time."

Elliott pulled hard at the door of the drinks cabinet, reaching inside for a tall glass bottle. Spinning the metal top off it, letting it fall to the floor, he lifted the neck of the bottle to his mouth and drank deeply. Almost greedily.

He hadn't drunk whisky since the day that Isobel had died. Now he would need it.

A small group of magpies chased each other among the branches of the fir trees, screeching, their noise harsh, almost brittle in the quiet shadows of the evening.

The men now stood together, the monk at their centre. The men who had walked across the fields and dusty tracks with the donkey. And those who had built the gibbet that now towered above them, its outline sharp against the deepening red skies.

A ladder stood against its wooden frame, reaching up to the cross-bar. Made of heavy, black mahogany, it had taken two men to carry it and to rest it against the beam.

The monk lifted his head, looking first out across the plains below, towards the dark shadow of the Atlantic and then slowly back towards the men who stood around him, the muscles of their faces taut, their lips unmoving. In the trees, the magpies still chattered and screeched. The wind still blew across the hard dusty surface of the hills and, in the half–light, along their sides, a figure now moved slowly.

The monk nodded towards two of the men. Emilio. The man with the scar. And another. Taller. Older.

"You."

Emilio hesitated. And then stepped forwards, followed by the older man.

Slowly they walked towards the donkey. The animal stood still. Its head no longer moved. Its ears flicked occasionally, warning off the small flies of the evening. Its eyes stared at the ground, as if dreaming.

Emilio reached the animal first, stretching out for the blanket, throwing it off, on to the ground. The body faced away from him, towards the bright cusp of the sun that was now disappearing behind the distant cliffs of Vilfeira. Its last glow caught the face of the body as Emilio now lifted it, cradling it in his arms, trying hard not to look down into the still, frightened eyes that stared at him. He could smell the *medronho*. Its effect would soon wear off.

He turned, the body limp in his arms, its feet and hands lashed together with rough cord. The second man stepped forward, holding out a hand. Emilio shook his head. He would carry the body alone. Slowly, he walked back towards the gibbet.

The monk had the knife in his hands. A broad silver blade, burnished in the glow of the skies above. As Emilio reached him, he lifted it, reaching out the hand that held it, touching the body.

Emilio stopped. The body he held was warm, as if still immersed in the heat of afternoon sun. The monk traced the point of the knife along its length, pausing as it reached the feet. Then swiftly, his hand blurring, he jerked the blade sideways, ripping the cord that held them, letting the legs fall free. And then cut the cord that bound the hands.

Now Emilio turned away, gazing up at the gibbet. Already one man had climbed the ladder and now sat on the cross-beam. Waiting. Others gathered round its base. And still none spoke.

The ropes were thrown, curling into the sky before dropping across the beam, trailing from it. Their ends were tied to the body's wrists and then quietly, as the magpies' chatter died with the coming of the night, the body was pulled up on to the wooden gibbet, the arms outstretched, finally fastened to the beam by the leather straps.

And, as the man who had fastened them now silently dropped to the ground, so the body began to swing from the gibbet in the warm evening air, the head hanging low on its shoulders.

"You stay here!"

"But Elliott, I. . ."

"There's no point in you going anywhere! I go. You stay."

Elliott slammed the glass down on the table. Too hard. A thin crack appeared in its side.

"Damn."

"Elliott, you can't drive like this."

"Then I'll walk."

"It's too far."

Elliott stood up, unsteady on his feet, his eyes reddening as the whisky began to take hold. For a moment the room seemed to move. Joaquim's voice seemed loud. Too loud.

"Why the hell are you shouting?"

"But I'm not. . ."

"Look, Joaquim. . ." Elliott stopped, aware

suddenly of what was happening. He picked up the glass and, walking slowly, deliberately, across the room, he dropped it into a small, tin wastebin. It shattered. He turned back towards Joaquim.

"Look, I'm forty eight. I'm old enough and stupid enough to know what I'm doing and neither you nor anyone else is going to stop me from going up there."

"But. . ."

Elliott raised his hand.

"Neither you nor anyone else."

He walked back across the room, picking up the keys for the jeep from the short, white mantelpiece. The half empty bottle still stood on the table. Elliott saw the metal top on the floor. Moving to it, bending down, he picked it up in his fingers, taking it to the bottle, screwing it in place.

"And you wait here. In case she comes back. Which she will." Elliott started walking towards the door, feeding the bottle into the deep pocket of his loose, canvas jacket. Reaching the door, he stopped, turning back.

"And tell me, Joaquim, how do I know that? Because I think I believe the policeman." He smiled. "This is all just a lousy waste of time."

The monk heard it first.

The sound of footsteps in the dirt. The small stones sent spinning down the hillside. The dried grass that splintered underfoot.

He waited, watching the girl's body swinging slowly in the soft winds of the evening. Then turned his gaze toward the tired, frightened faces of the men who stood beneath it.

"Do you hear it?"

His voice was quiet. No one spoke as each man listened, their senses picking out each bustle of wings in the branches of the trees, each bird call from the deepening shadows of the evening.

"There!"

The monk turned sharply, jerking his arm into the air, pointing towards the slope of the hill behind him.

"In Spiritus!"

The frightened, widening eyes of the men around him followed the movement, each man's skin cold, his muscles tightening, fear crawling through his body as the figure slowly emerged from the dusk.

Shoulders hunched, the footsteps slow across the broken ground. The blur of the face that now lifted towards them, the two eyes that now held them in their gaze.

Emilio spoke first, his voice the whisper of relief.

"Joao."

The flames were bright against the shadowed outline of the hills, their sides lit only by the pale phosphorescence of the starlight and the early pallor of the rising moon.

Elliott was sweating, his hands slipping as he flung the wheel from side to side, struggling with the bucking, rearing jeep as he hurled it across the rutted ground. Here, at the foot of the hills, there were no longer roads. Simply the tracks left by the feet of animals scouring the hillsides for food and for shelter from the sun.

The jeep lurched violently to the left as Elliott braked hard, jamming his foot to the floor, grabbing at the wheel as the headlights raked across the thin line of olive trees he had seen with seconds to spare.

His vision was blurring, images of the night flickering at the edges of his mind, his sense of direction held only by the light of the torches glittering in the hills above.

The whisky burned in his stomach. Waves of nausea swept through his body, feeding on the bile that swelled at the back of his throat. Frequently, he would shake his head viciously, as if trying to rid himself of the dull aching that was now wound about his brain.

The ground was steeper.

At each side, the shadows were fewer, the tangled, twisted groves of trees and the jumbled fields of untidy, tall grasses having long given way to the bare, scorched earth of the hillsides.

And still the flames burned, their light closer now.

Elliott drove faster, pushing the vehicle across

the shale and gravel, listening to the screaming of the engine as it echoed across the darkened hills.

There were figures. People. Shadows that stood beside the flames. Images drifting in and out of Elliott's mind. He stared at them, desperately trying to sharpen the outlines of what he saw, fighting the jeep as it slithered across ground that was now flattening, sweeping towards the small cluster of pines, the circle of torches and the ruins of the monastery beyond.

Elliott grabbed at the gear-stick, jerking it back, kicking the brake pedal, forcing the thick rubber of the tyres to bite hard into the sun-burnt earth, throwing up a thick cloud of dust into the air.

He reached for the key. Flicked it. The engine died.

And the silence of the evening followed, broken only by the crackle of the flames burning the greased, wooden bundles of the torches.

Slowly, unsteadily, Elliott climbed out of the jeep, his gaze now turning towards the tall wooden gibbet, the men who stood beneath it and the shadowed body of the girl that hung from it.

He moved round the back of the jeep, running his hand along its side, as if to steady himself as he walked. Emilio he recognized. And Joao. And the monk, who stood quite still, his eyes following Elliott, his face bathed in the bright, orange glare of the flames.

Finally, Elliott left the jeep and began to walk across the dry, uneven ground. Beyond the circle of torchlight, the hills lay in darkness. His vision blurred. He rubbed his eyes with the back of his hands, stumbling, lifting his head again almost as if in surprise that the vision had not faded. That he was not alone among the hills of the Algarve. Walking through the shadows, listening to the soft sounds of the night.

None of them spoke as he moved towards them. Some shifted back into the shadows, outside the circle. Others looked towards the ground. Only the monk held Elliott in his gaze, watching him as he stopped and slowly looked up towards the girl. From a distance, her face had been shadowed. Elliott now saw her quite clearly.

"Denny?"

13

The moon was high.

At first, Denny hadn't realized what she was looking at. Three white fragments of a circle slowly fusing into one. A half-moon. Floating in the deep Algarvean sky, leaning on its back, spilling moonlight across the darkened corners of the Earth.

She could feel her fingers. She could move them. But her wrists were held. Moving her head, glancing along the length of her outstretched arms, she could see the leather straps. Holding her to the beam. Like the moon, she seemed to be floating, her body moving slowly in the warm, light wind of the night.

She could smell woodsmoke. Looking down, she

could see the embers of what had once been torches, now thrown on to the ground where their flames had slowly died. She couldn't touch the ground. She hung above it, the dust and stones beyond her reach.

And then she understood. In this dream, she had left her body. She had become a spirit, free to wander through the skies, to fly with the birds, to circle the clouds with the lonely sequoia.

But her arms. Numbed. Tied with thick leather straps to the wooden beam. Holding her above the ground. And the bitter-sweet taste of strawberries at the back of her mouth. And the nagging pain across the roof of her skull. They didn't belong to such a dream. And the shadows that she could now see, moving among the glowing embers, staying at the edges of the moonlight that washed across the ground. People. People perhaps come to wake her. To shake her from her dream. Spectres from the edges of her imagination come to bring the news of daybreak and to break the spells woven by the world of sleep.

But they didn't come. They stayed at the edges of the light. Denny shook her head. She pulled at the straps and began to kick her legs, hopelessly, as if riding an invisible bicycle through the air. And each time she swung her body forwards, so she then fell back, cracking the knuckled vertebrae of her backbone against the stiff wooden pole that stood behind her, supporting the beam.

She began to scream. At first whimpering. Then crying. Then screaming into the night. The shrill, hopeless sound of terror that echoed through the hills and then died. And as tears began to run across the skin of her face, so the man appeared below her. Dressed in a gown, his head bared to the moonlight, his eyes cold.

"You are the only woman left in your family. She will come for you. And for your body."

The voice was hoarse. Low. Unkind.

"Help me. Help me, please."

Denny struggled to speak, her throat burning, scarred by the medronho they had forced her to drink.

"It will soon be over."

"Please!" Denny screamed. "Please help me!"

The monk let the last traces of her words melt into the night, letting the silence of the hillside return. And then spoke, raising his hand slowly.

"In Spiritus."

He turned and walked back into the shadows, joining the *mordomos* who stood in silence, waiting.

The girl on the beam was quiet again. They had seen her fear, heard the screams that had eaten into the very core of their souls. For a moment, Joao had wanted to run forward, to climb the pole, to cut the straps. But Emilio had stopped him. And now the two men stood together, looking into the shadows that circled them, listening.

The figure appeared to their right. Silently. At first, no more than a tall shadow, moving, almost drifting, across the ground. Coming in from the pines, towards the group of men and the girl hanging from the gibbet above them. Moving more quickly as it came closer, it took the shape of a woman, her face pale in the moonlight, her long dark hair framing its hollowed contours. As she closed on them, so her cloak dropped from her shoulders and, lifting her head towards the stars, she began a low moaning sound that grew in intensity as she neared. A moan that grew to a shriek. And that stopped as the figure now paused before the men.

Some did not look. Others let their eyes turn towards the lobisomen, looking for the first time at the woman with no eyes and the body she had stolen. Slowly, the creature moved past them, its face now turned upwards towards the girl hanging from the beam. Again, the moan. The low, gurgling sound of blood rising in the throat. The sudden movement, the shriek and the blur as the creature hurled itself upwards, clutching at the girl, burying its face in her neck.

And then falling back to the ground, to lie as if in death; the black peasant clothes it had worn now a funeral shawl, billowing gently in the warm night winds of the Algarve.

14

Joaquim watched as the first thin stripes of the dawn began to trace the skies to the east. He hadn't slept. All night he had waited for Elliott. And for Denny. Sitting on the quiet, darkened patio, listening to the cicadas and the animals of the night.

Sitting by the table where he and Denny had talked of dreams. And of the young girl who came to Joaquim in the night, the words she spoke, the hand she waved in farewell.

And then he had seen the girl again. Standing in the gardens in front of him. And this time, he had heard the word. The word she whispered over and over again.

"Denny."

And Joaquim had stood up and begun to walk

towards her. But she had gone, leaving only the sounds and shadows of the night.

And long after she had disappeared, Joaquim sat by the table and tried to understand what he had seen. And what he had heard.

The air around him now began to warm as the early morning sun climbed slowly into the sky, burning off the thin ribbons of mist that drifted across the gardens and among the tall pines. He stood up, turning and then walking into the villa through the open patio doors. He almost expected to see them. Denny running down the stairs, Elliott emerging from his study, his English newspaper tucked under his arm. But the rooms were empty.

Joaquim crossed to the front door, opening it. His mother would know. Or his father, Joao. They would tell him that the stories were nonsense. That the only reason Elliott hadn't come back was because he was almost certainly in a ditch, reeking of whisky, his jeep bent beyond repair. And Denny? She might even be with him.

He pushed his bike slowly up the short drive and on to the thin dusty road that ran past the villa. He climbed on to it, flicking the ignition switch, kicking the starter. The engine growled into life. Looking up, Joaquim turned the machine toward Vilfeira and, easing the throttle back, began to move slowly away from the villa.

*   *   *

The village was quiet.

There had been an old man walking by the roadside, pushing a small, hand-made cart, filled with clothing. He had waved as Joaquim had passed him. The rag man. He came to the village every Saturday morning. A woman had been scrubbing the white stone of her doorstep, so intent on her work that she had not even noticed the motorbike. And a cyclist, wobbling towards him on the other side of the road on a bicycle that might have fallen to pieces at any moment.

Their front door was open. But nobody sat on the stone bench outside.

Joaquim pulled up beside the small cottage, leaning the bike against its wall. For a moment, he hesitated, thinking that he heard the sound of someone crying. And then turned and walked slowly through the door.

It was dark inside the cottage, the curtains of the small windows still closed against the night, the rooms lit only by the soft glow of the early morning sunlight that spilled through the door. Sofia sat by the fire, its embers long dead, the smell of the burning wood now no more than a scent in the air.

"*Mama?*"

His mother turned quickly, her eyes widening almost as if in disbelief, the tears once more running down her cheeks. She stood up, quickly, stumbling across the shadows of the small room, reaching for her son, throwing her arms around his neck, burying her face in his shoulder, her body suddenly limp, the sense of despair now one of relief.

It was some moments before she spoke. When she did, her voice was low, thickened by the hours spent crying by the fire, watching as it died.

"I thought they must have taken you too."

She looked up at him, her arms still around him, the tears in her eyes blurring the sight of her son.

"Who, Mama?"

"The same people that took the girl."

She slowly turned away from him and sat at the small wooden table in the centre of the room, clasping her hands together on its surface.

"The *mordomos*?" said Joaquim.

His mother nodded.

"Do you know what the last thing was your father said to me before he left? When I shrieked at him that he was a fool. And now a murderer. Do you know what the stupid man said?"

Joaquim shook his head.

"He said he was sorry."

Sofia almost spat the words from her mouth, turning away again from her son.

"The idiot said he was sorry."

"But I thought he said the monk was mad. That he was having no more to do with it."

There was an anxiety now in Joaquim's voice, a

tightness in his throat. His mother looked up, the tears drying on her skin, her words almost ones of resignation.

"And do you know what the most stupid thing is, Joaquim? The real madness? The idiots honestly think they're burning a witch."

He was going too fast. On the uneven surface of the country road the bike would rear and twist as its wheels hammered into each crack, each jagged hole.

Joaquim clung to the machine. Beneath him, the bike's frame shook violently, threatening to shatter, to scar the ground with burnt, twisted metal and with the body of its young rider. And yet Joaquim kept the throttle jammed back, the knuckles of his hand white as he gripped the steering bars, his eyes fixed on the hills now beginning to loom above him.

He hadn't seen the donkey.

A *burro*. Ambling across the ground, its head stooped to the earth, its teeth pulling at the patchy, yellow grass. It recognized no difference as it now moved from the fields to the edges of the road. It could hear the noise. The noise that was growing louder. But it was just a noise. Noises came and went.

Spinning grit high into the air, Joaquim swerved the bike to the right as the track bent sharply round the edges of a small crop of olive trees. He jammed the brakes on, throwing the back wheel to the left, briefly out of control. And then pulled hard at the throttle, hurling the bike forwards again, blistering through the rising curtain of dust.

The animal looked up at the last moment.

Seeing the shadow rearing out of the sun towards him, hearing the roar of the engine, watching as it now spun viciously away, howling and exploding in a ball of flame as it hit the trees.

And then the silence returned.

And leaving the road, the donkey began to pick once again at the worn grass of the plains.

The water felt good.

Cold, running across his face. Washing away the grit and the blood that ran from the cut across his forehead.

"I seem to be making a habit of finding bodies."

The voice was soft.

Joaquim's eyes flickered open, the bright sunlight of the afternoon partially obscured by the silhouette that knelt over him, letting the water fall from a small, stone pitcher.

"I. . ."

"Don't talk. Not yet."

"But. . ."

Joaquim was sitting, leaning against the soft trunk of an olive tree which he now used as a support as he struggled painfully to his feet.

"You don't understand."

"Ah," said the shepherd. "But I think I do. And I think you may be too late."

Joaquim glanced at the smouldering remains of the bike, the twisted metal, the heavy engine casing half-buried in the earth.

"Someone saved me."

"Yes," said the shepherd. "Someone did."

Joaquim turned back to him.

"Then at least I have to try."

The shepherd smiled briefly. Then stooped to the ground, spreading his right hand across it, gathering a handful of the dry, rust-brown soil. He straightened again, holding his hand out to Joaquim. Too many people had been hurt.

"Then you will need this."

It was too late for the girl. But the boy might survive.

The chamber was damp. Outside, they knew the sun would be shining, burning the ground, drying the grasses. But deep in the hillside, standing beneath the ruins of the monastery, the men gathered in the half-light felt only the chill of the cold stone that surrounded them.

Joao had lost any real sense of time.

Dawn had been breaking when they had taken the girl down from the beam, their ears deaf to the sound of her hideous screams. She had twisted in the grip of their hands, spat at them, shrieked as the Algarvean skies had begun to redden, as if awash with the blood of the creature's victims.

And, as silhouettes burnt into the rich fabric of the sky, the sequoia had flown in circles, slowly drifting high above their heads as the men had finally carried their blood-soaked quarry into the hills. And now she lay on the stone table. Her wrists and ankles held by the thick leather straps. Her body quite still, lit by the orange glow of the torch burning at the head of the table. Joao tried hard not to look at her eyes.

The monk was speaking softly to himself, almost unaware of the men who watched him from the shadows. Joao had leant forwards, trying to hear the words, to understand what the man was saying. To make some sense out of the woman's body that lay outside. And that of the girl who now lay at the centre of the dim light, her eyelids closed, her breathing slight.

He had heard the words. But he had not understood them. They were not words that he had ever heard before.

Somewhere, water was dripping, the sound echoing through the long dark corridor that had led them to the chamber. Past the coffins. Past the broken skull that had stared back at Joao through the broken, rotting wooden boards that had once protected it. Past the slow-moving, dark waters of the stream that ran through the caves and that had once run thick with blood from the tables.

The monk had stopped speaking.

He now stood at the base of the table, looming over the body of the girl. He was reaching above his head, his hand rising, his fingers curling about the handle of the broad, glittering knife that hung there. The knife with the claw at its tip. The knife that cut the flesh of its victims and then tore it from their bones.

With a twist of his hand, he pulled it free of the rope from which it had hung and now he stood above the girl, the knife held high in the air, fatty beads of sweat pulsing down the sides of his thin, sallow face. His eyes narrowed.

No one spoke. None moved. Joao had told them of Manuel. Had whispered to them during the night, as they watched the girl screaming from the wooden beam, that Manuel was dead, his face hideously contorted by the final moments of his death, the scars of the snake-bites livid weals on the skin of his neck. They had crossed the line, at one side of which the monk and his ways had been no more than the conjuring tricks of a clown. But at this side, they were now the cause of death and the raising of the horrors of the spirit world.

"In Spiritus."

The monk said the words slowly, quietly, holding

the knife with both hands, still glittering above his head in the sputtering light of the torch.

"In Spiritus."

This time louder, the sound bitter, the voice speaking of the hatred of centuries.

"In Spiritus."

The girl's eyelids flickered, opening to reveal the black hollows behind. She began to jerk her limbs, pulling viciously against the straps, writhing at the sight of the knife and at the sound of the words hissed by the monk. She screamed, howling, the shrill pain of her voice burning through the minds of the men who now cowered in the shadows, their senses numbed by the hideous cacophony of sound conjured up from the deepest pits of Hell.

"In Spiritus!"

The monk was shouting the words, twitching the knife, the veins at the sides of his head thick with the blood that pounded through them.

"In Spiritus!"

"No! No! Denny!"

And suddenly silence fell on the chamber, the echoes of the screams and the murderous, bellowed chanting of the monk dying into the dark corners, falling slowly against the harsh, glistening stone of the walls. And Joaquim slowly walked forwards, broaching the small circle of light, his clothes bloody, his face streaked with sweat and the dust of the plains.

"Joaquim, I—"

"Shut up!"

Joaquim ignored his father, not taking his eyes off the monk, aware only of the girl lashed to the stone table, her eyes hollow, her face twisted by the evil buried deep beneath the skin.

"Madman! What in God's name—"

"You fool."

The words were low, almost spat into Joaquim's taut face.

"Behold! The lobisomen!"

And the monk suddenly twisted, raising the knife, bringing it down viciously, hacking into the leg of the girl, sinking the blade deep into her flesh. And then lifted it again, turning, almost smiling, his eyes bitter, his voice contemptuous.

"You see. Now there is no blood."

Joaquim had seen his father's face at the window. Briefly. Looking through the cold steel bars at his son. Then glancing away quickly, as if in fear of discovery. And he had heard the sound of the key in the door being turned, the slow rasp of the metal as the lock was carefully prised open.

His father had looked back at him again, and had drawn the imagined sign of the cross across his chest. And then had gone, the sound of his footsteps fading as he had hurried back to the chamber.

And now Joaquim sat alone.

The sound of the *mordomos* had long disappeared. And with them, the screaming of the girl. Denny. Denny with no eyes. With no blood. Her screams had stopped suddenly, as if silenced. Then Joaquim remembered the knife. And the blades of the guillotines that hung quietly over the tables.

He stood up, his body aching from the crash. And from the violent, desperate scramble up the sides of the hills, the skin of his legs torn by the dried grass and brambles, his fingernails broken by the stones of the ground as he had finally crawled beneath the tall, wooden beam and into the dark hollows of the caves beyond it.

But the shepherd had been right. He had been too late.

He began to move towards the door. And, as his hand closed on the thick wooden handle, so one of the snakes fell noiselessly to the ground, the thick circles of its stomach muscles rippling beneath its dry skin as it began to move across the cold stone floor.

The corridor was dark, its shadows lit only by the gleam of the torch that still burned in the chamber beyond. Joaquim moved quietly, pausing, listening.

There was no sound. Save for the sputtering of the torch, the animal fat that coated its thin wooden tapers spitting, as it melted in the glare of its flames. As he edged slowly forwards, Joaquim looked ahead, his eyes searching the shadows for signs of movement. The hand that reached for his throat. The face that reared up like the bull before it died, its heart pierced by the lance of the matador. Or the sudden appearance of the monk at his side, his eyes glittering as he whispered the word, "fool".

He left the corridor, moving slowly into the chamber.

It was empty. The table that had held Denny was bare, the leather straps untied, hanging loosely at its sides. Above, the thin merciless edges of the guillotine blades still glistened in the torchlight, held there by the thick rope that ran to the stone floor behind.

Joaquim moved across the floor. There was something on the ground, beside the tables. As he drew closer, he could see that it was the knife the monk had used. Thrown carelessly down on to the stones. Perhaps there had been no more need for it.

Standing beside the table, Joaquim bent to pick it up, his fingers curling round its thick, silver handle. It felt cold. As he held it in the light of the flames, the letters engraved in its bright, broad blade were clear. The same as those carved into the dark marble of the tables.

I.S.

In Spiritus. The chant of the monk.

Joaquim remembered the stories. The innocents of the Algarve who had been slaughtered by the monks in their search for the lobisomen. He wondered how many had died, the blade of this knife cutting savagely at their skin.

He threw it viciously into the shadows beyond the tables. The shrill clatter of metal against stone echoing through the deep shadows of the caves, finally dying, buried beneath the silence that now returned.

There was a movement. So slight, so subtle, that it might have been the flickering of the torch against the chamber walls. Joaquim turned, looking back towards the corridor. Across the floor, there seemed to be a long, dark line. Quite still. The shadow of the rope that held the guillotine.

Joaquim turned back to the table, to the torch at its head. He would need it to find his way out. It seemed to be held in place with thin twine. He began to work at the twine with his fingers, pulling, at it, snatching, working the ends of it loose.

And then he realized.

The guillotine rope hung behind the flame. Not in front. It had not been its shadow that had crossed the floor.

He turned quickly. The creature had scaled the side of the table and its neck was now rising quickly above it, the green shale of its skin glowing in the light of the flames. Holding its head high, its small, black eyes fastened on Joaquim, the thick muscles of its stomach pulling its long, tapering body on to the table, the mamba curled its neck, its head slightly thrown back, the final moment of grace before it struck, the last image of the world for its victim.

Joaquim grabbed the torch, shaking it, twisting it, trying to break it free, to hurl it at the snake, to burn the creature. A twine snapped. The torch loosened. Desperately, violently, Joaquim pulled at it. The snake's head was steadying, its tongue flickering, its jaws breaking open.

"*Then you will need this.*"

The shepherd's words. The soil. Joaquim pushed his hand into his pocket, grabbing at the dry, acidic soil of the plains, pulling it out, hurling it at the snake's head.

It was enough.

The earth in its face, the creature reared away, temporarily blinded, the pain biting at the nerve-ends behind its eyes. It threw itself forward, flattening against the face of the marble table, thrashing its head from side to side.

And then died as the blade of the guillotine hammered into the table, slicing through the snake's backbone and body, spilling its blood and standing proud above it as both halves of the creature slowly rolled on to the stone of the floor.

"I couldn't do it any earlier. It would have seen me."

The voice was halting, whispered, broken. But recognizable. Joaquim turned quickly.

"Elliott."

High above, against the deep black velvet of the Algarvean night-time skies, the rockets exploded, their blast seeming to shake the very foundations of the town's buildings. Shimmering waves of sparks, incandescent, burning, multi-coloured, spread like fans across the sky, holding the world in their gaze for one moment, before burning out and falling noiselessly to the ground. And music. Loud, raucous, angry music.

The music of a people whose history had been to scratch a living from the bare soil of the plains. A people born into poverty, with little hope of an easy life and with every expectation of an early death.

Throughout Vilfeira, the whirling, jangling, incessant rhythms of songs, written by people whose names had been long forgotten, coursed through the shifting, tumbling, swirling crowds that now jammed the streets. The small children who ran screeching from one corner to another, their faces streaked with sweat, their eyes bright with excitement. The farmers who bellowed obscenities and greetings above the heads of their neighbours, waving their hands furiously, sometimes spinning their flat, woollen caps high into the air, careless of where they might fall. The hooting, delirious shrieking of the drunks who clutched at each other's shoulders and staggered like so many stick-insects across the uneven cobbles of the road. The crazed, weaving patterns of a crowd that shouted, sang and screamed with laughter beneath the crash of the fireworks above, and that glowed with excitement, each face bathed in the deep orange glare of the torches. Torches that had now been lit, their flames reaching into the sky, their brilliance dulling the strings of smaller party lights that swung from the windows and doorways of the town.

The torches that would mark the route of the procession.

"We're all right while they're still letting off fireworks!"

Elliott was shouting, pitching his voice above the howl of the jeep's engine and the whirl of the night-time air as it span past the open cockpit.

Joaquim looked across at him, gripping the edges of the windscreen, bracing his body against the tumbling, yawing movement of the jeep as it closed on the outlines of the town ahead. It had been many years since he had gone to the procession.

"I don't understand!"

Elliott swung the wheel violently to his left. And

then straightened again, his eyes never leaving the shadows of the road ahead.

"The fireworks! They won't start the procession till they've finished the display!"

Joaquim looked back towards the town again. Still the sky above it glowed as the myriad splinters of light from the exploding shells scattered across it.

They could hear the music. The waves of sound drifting towards them, jumbled, confused, inarticulate.

The countryside had been deserted. Each small village, each shabby clutch of white-washed cottages empty, save for the dogs that would leap from the roadside and chase the jeep as it passed, barking furiously. Or the chickens that ran screeching into the bushes, beating their wings against their sides. Or the old man they had seen at a small roadside bar, his gaunt frame silhouetted against the dull candle-light that spilled from the open door behind him.

Someone had beaten Elliott. The ugly gash running down the side of his face hadn't happened because he'd fallen over. Even if he had been drunk. Joaquim guessed it must have been the monk.

He looked back to the road. No more than five minutes.

They could see the rooftops of the town

now, one moment in shadow, the next in brilliant light as yet another series of explosions brought a cascade of glittering stars to the skies above them.

Elliott swung the wheel to the right, turning the jeep off the road, pushing it now along a thin dusty track that seemed to wind its way towards the northern edges of the town.

"The streets will be jammed! The only chance we've got is to dump this thing and come down through the *Laberinto*."

Joaquim nodded.

O Laberinto. A tangled labyrinth of narrow, rotting alleyways. Gutted by fire and by disease over the centuries. Once the home of the very poorest, built to house those made destitute by the earthquakes that had destroyed the monastery. Now no more than broken-walled, roofless tenements, a home only for the town's rats.

The north side was deserted. Both Elliott and Joaquim knew the procession started in the south of the town, working its way through the crowded streets toward the towering pyramid of dried wood in the market square. It would take half an hour, maybe more. They had time.

"Elliott!"

Joaquim spoke as the jeep slewed to a halt in the dust, facing the windowless, broken walls of the *Laberinto*.

Elliott killed the engine, pulling himself out of his seat. He turned back towards Joaquim.

"What?"

"Look."

Joaquim was pointing towards the sky. A sky that was suddenly dark, above a town that had now grown quiet.

"The rockets. They've stopped."

They moved slowly.

Each step taken as if to the sound of an unseen drum. Laboured. Deliberate. The cage was heavy. For each of the men who carried it, there was now the memory of the years before. The ache that sharpened slowly into pain, as the wooden bars of the cage began to chafe their shoulders, rubbing slowly at first, tearing at the threads of their shirts, breaking the skin and finally hollowing a bloody weal in their flesh that would later harden into a broad, livid scar.

As they walked, the body hanging in the cage rocked slowly from side to side.

They neared the first of the torches that stood proudly at the sides of the narrow, cobbled streets, seeing the first shadows of the crowd that would line the way to the square. Silent faces. No words of acclaim. No thoughts of applause. There would be no cheering until they brought the cage into the square and the tall pyre, at last, was lit.

Joao looked straight ahead.

He and Emilio had taken the front, each at one corner. Joao had said it was because he needed to show his faith in the monk after his moments of doubt. It had not been true. He had wanted to walk in front so that he could not see the girl's body as he carried her to a certain death.

He thought of Joaquim. The boy would have heard him turn the key in the lock, opening the door. He would have waited. And then found his way out of the caves. Perhaps now he would be at home. Safe. And he thought of Elliott. The man they had left lying on the floor of the chamber. Drunk. Unconscious. Whom the monk had kicked savagely on the side of the head. Perhaps he was dead.

The crowds were bigger now, jammed against the walls and windows of the small shops and houses of the town, gazing at the cage and the figure inside it. The effigy of the lobisomen. The dummy that was burnt on the fire to the cheers of the crowds in a celebration of one of the oldest and most unpleasant legends of the Algarve.

They waited as it passed. Then slowly spilled out on to the road behind it, following the procession. Sometimes the children would whisper to each other, or giggle behind the safety of their mother's skirt. But all followed the cage, almost as if pushing it through the streets of the town.

Joao's shoulder was hurting. The shirt he wore

212

was made of thick cloth, too warm for the heat of a summer's night and yet some protection against the splinters and chafing of the cage. But it had torn. And now the wood was beginning to burn his skin, pressing hard against the bones that moved beneath it.

He glanced sideways at Emilio. The man was breathing hard, his face beginning to twist as the strain of the cage they carried increased.

They turned into the Rua Escura, a short cobbled street that grubbed its way upwards towards the Rua da Galacia: the longer, wider road that led finally into the square. There were no torches on the Rua Escura, the cobbles lit only by the glow that spilled from those ahead.

Joao turned again to look at his friend. And then, instinctively, he looked up. The body was shadowed, briefly hidden from the glare of the torches. And yet Joao had seen the movement. Where once it had done no more than swing gently from the hook and the leather straps that held it, the body had now begin to stiffen.

And, in the shadows of the Rua Escura, Joao saw the head turn towards him.

They heard the cheers first. The wild, hysterical screaming and baying of the crowd as they saw the cage and the *mordomos* turn into the Rua da Galacia. Within sight of the fire. The massive pyramid of dried wood that suddenly burst into tall, jagged, bright orange flames, twisting into the night sky, clawing their way rapidly up the side of the pyre.

"We're too late!" screamed Joaquim.

"No, we're not! Keep going!"

Elliott clutched his chest as he ran, pressing hard against the pain there.

They could both see the glow of the fire in the sky, the sparks whirling in the smoke, high above the roofs of the houses that surrounded the square. As they ran, they could hear the howls of the crowd growing louder. Trumpets were being blown. Crazily. Out of tune.

"We're. . ."

"Shut up and run!"

Elliott bellowed the words, almost as if in hope that the buildings around them would fall to the ground, burying the cheers of the crowd, and the fire that burnt before them. His heart hammered against his chest.

The first bullet missed him, the blast of the gun deafening in the narrow alleyway. Elliott turned, hurling himself against the wall, twisting to see the police captain lifting the gun again, straightening his arm.

"Elliott!"

"Run!"

Elliott shrieked the word, suddenly zig-zagging furiously across the narrow road.

"Run! Damn you!"

A second bullet crashed down the alley, hacking into the rough plaster of the walls behind Elliott. Joaquim ran. Hurling himself along the thin pavement, bouncing against the walls, tearing the skin of his shoulders. Not turning to see Elliott, listening only to the crack of the gun and the whine of the bullets as they missed Elliott's twisting, weaving shadow.

And then the scream.

Joaquim threw himself to the ground, bundling his body across the rough cobbles, reaching for the safety of the corner, turning it and flattening himself against the wall, gasping for air, sucking it greedily into his mouth.

And looked back.

The captain was now running up the alley, shouting. Elliott was on the ground.

"Elliott!"

Again, the gun fired, its lead slug chipping the bricks above Joaquim's head. He turned quickly away, pitching himself forwards, and began to run desperately across the edge of the square. The bellows, the shouts, the cheers and the screams of the crowd now hitting him in the face, the brilliant glare of the torches and the pitiless cauldron of the towering fire now reaching out towards him, welcoming him to the party as Joaquim flung himself into the safety of the shifting, heaving, tangled mass, escaping from the gun.

And from the thought of Elliott's body in the dirt of the alley, slowly dying.

It was almost impossible to move quickly. But Joao knew they must. Already, he could feel the movement through the wood. The signs that the creature was beginning to pull at the straps that held her. Beginning to kick, to tug.

In the chaos that now surrounded them, the shouting, whistling, jeering crowd, no one would notice that the dummy was moving. They would assume it was no more than the cage shaking, toppling from side to side as the twelve *mordomos* desperately clawed their way along the Rua da Galacia, their pace ever quicker, their steps shorter.

Increasingly, the monk looked back towards them, staring up at the cage, his eyes without emotion in the glare of the torches and of the fire that grew ever taller in the square ahead. Irritated, he made short, jabbing movements with his hand, cursing them, urging them on like so many oxen in a field.

And, as they now approached it, so the noise in the square became deafening.

The hideous shrieking of trumpets. The crash of the rockets once again tearing into the night sky only to explode in brilliant shards of light. The howling, roaring, screaming voices building walls of sound that now began to crush against the exhausted, sweating men, staggering beneath the weight of the cage and their victim.

"Let me through! Out of the way! For pity's sake!"

Above the deafening roar, the monk heard the voice. The voice of the boy. He couldn't see him. In such chaos, in such madness, it was impossible. Amongst the teeming, twisting, screaming faces, burnished in the glare of the fire like so many demons from the deepest pits of Hell, no one person could ever be seen.

The monk glanced back again, shouting now, his voice thick with the sense of fear. The fear of failure. No other.

As he ran, stumbling, he knew that even if he had to drag the creature from the straps himself and bury it deep in the flames, then he would do so with no fear. The pain of being burnt alive no more than the price to be paid for the death of the lobisomen.

"Let me through!"

Again, the scream of the boy.

"Emilio! Papa!"

The monk stared frantically into the crowd. Then back at the *mordomos*.

"Move!"

Staggering, bleeding, terrified, the mordomos stumbled drunkenly to the edge of the fire, deafened now by the roar of the flames and the howling of the mob beyond. The fire's heat burnt into their flesh, its brilliance seared into the backs of their eyes. And the cage they held began to shake furiously, the creature inside now throwing its body from side to side.

"Papa! It's Denny!"

Joaquim had burst through the edges of the crowd, and was standing at the edge of the fire, his dirty, blood-streaked face bright in the flames.

"Denny! Do you hear?"

He screamed the words, as if trying to shake his father loose from his apparent madness.

"Back, fool!"

The monk grabbed at Joaquim. The boy swung round viciously, hammering his fist into the side of the man's head.

"Cabrao!"

The monk dropped slowly to his knees, his hands to his face, as if in prayer. Joaquim turned back to the cage, now rocking from side to side.

Joao felt the pain in his shoulder as the cage moved across the edges of his bone, felt the blood seeping through the cloth of his shirt. It was breaking. The wood was breaking. Above him, the wood of the cage was splintering. As the screams of the crowd rose to a pitch that seemed to shake the very corners of the earth, so Joao knew that the cage was opening, the wood breaking, the creature screaming.

"Papa!"

Joaquim stared as the cage collapsed on top of the *mordomos*, the thick wooden bars crumbling like so many matchsticks. He heard the screams of the men who died beneath it. Saw the body fall to the ground.

And, suddenly, there was silence.

Where moments earlier, chaos had taken the square to the edges of insanity, now nothing moved, no one spoke. The only sound, the flames of the fire and the cracking of the wood that they burned.

And in the centre of the square stood the girl.

Frail, her long, dark hair ruffled by the light wind that now blew, she said nothing. Joaquim had seen her before. He had seen her in his dreams. The girl who waved to him. And who disappeared when he spoke.

For some moments, the girl stood quite still and then, almost as if guided by an unseen hand, she walked slowly towards the shattered cage.

The flames of the fire threw her shadow across the square, reaching out to the silent faces of the people who stood quietly at its edges, watching in silence as the girl now stopped. And raised her hand, lifting it towards the wreckage, as if in invitation to a dance.

"It is time."

Her voice was quiet and yet all in the square heard it. Like the soft chimes of the Tibetan bell, blowing in the winds of the mountainside.

And slowly a figure emerged from the splintered wooden bars and the shadows of the bodies they covered. Standing slowly. A tall, thin figure. It moved slowly towards the girl, its yellow skin now visible in the firelight. The furled layers of skin that fell away from the outline of its skeleton. The high bones of its cheeks. The black holes where once there had been eyes. The long black hair and the torn, ragged thin cloths that hung over the desiccated flesh. The head held high. Proud. Strong. The trace of a smile on its lips. The thin, tapering fingers of its hands now reaching out towards the girl. Taking her hand and slowly following as she turned and walked towards the fire.

And still the square was silent.

As the girl neared the edge of the fire, she stopped, looking across at Joaquim. And suddenly, quietly, he understood. And lifted his head, slowly.

"Will she be all right?"

The girl nodded.

"Yes."

Joaquim listened to the flames, beginning to burn more fiercely as the wind caught them.

"What shall I tell her?"

The girl looked carefully at Joaquim.

"That I love her." And then she smiled. "And that God laid the bricks in Kinsale."

She raised her hand, as if in farewell, talking softly.

"In Spiritus."

And then, slowly, she walked into the fire, taking the gaunt, blinded figure with her.

And as the smoke from the fire curled upwards into the velvet, star-lit skies of the Algarve, so it blew neither to the right, nor to the left. But drifted slow and straight, towards the dark shadows of the birds that flew above. Noiselessly circling the town and the burning pyre at its centre.

And the silent faces that looked upwards towards the broad wings of the sequoia.

15

As dawn broke, its first glow bringing life to the darkened shapes and angles of the buildings that stood at the edges of the square, so the Levanter wind began again to blow from the east, scratching the dust across the cobbles and flat stones of the Plaza Vilfeira. Picking up the torn, crumpled, coloured streamers that had once flown proudly from the windows and galleries of the town's buildings but which were now no more than scraps of paper, swirling in tight eddies, as the wind chased them through the half-light of the early morning.

The square was almost empty.

The crowds had long since disappeared, melting hurriedly, almost ashamed, into the night. The echoes of their shrieking, their shouting, their applause were gone, leaving only the wind and the occasional barking of a dog to add presence to the growing light of the day.

They sat in the centre of the square. Unmoving. Their arms about each other, providing warmth in the chill of the dark watches of the night and now strength in the face of what the new day might bring. Denny's leg hurt. The knife-wound had been deep. Joaquim had torn the sleeve off his shirt and tied it tightly round her leg, slowing the flow of the blood, easing the pain.

It still hurt. But it meant that she was alive.

Beside the pool at the centre of the square, the embers of the fire still burned. The spitting, cascading pyramid of flame that only hours before had seemed to burn the very edges of Heaven now reduced to the occasional spark, fanned gently by the wind, sent tumbling and spinning from the blackened stumps of wood.

"Elliott was lucky," said Joaquim quietly.

"I suppose we all were." Denny was looking across the square, watching as the skies began to lighten. She was surprised how quickly the dawn was breaking. "It didn't really happen, Joaquim. Did it?"

Joaquim looked at her, the blue eyes bright in the early light of the day, the long dark hair thrown back over her shoulders.

"I don't know."

In the distance, he thought he could hear the jeep's engine. Elliott would be driving slowly, nursing his way through the shadows of the town's silent streets, the bullet in his shoulder painful but better there than in his head.

He had been lucky. The police captain had not come back.

Behind them lay the body of the monk. As the crowds had backed slowly away from the fire, he had fallen, curling slowly to the ground, wrapping himself in the robes he wore, the cowl dropping over his head, his body burying itself in the threadbare folds of the cloth.

During the night he had not moved.

As Joaquim and Denny had held each other through the night, the fire slowly burning to the ground, the monk had been their only company. The bodies of the *mordomos* had long gone. Those who had survived had been helped from the square, clutching at the rescuers' shoulders, limping into the shadows with no thought to look back. Those who had died had simply been carried into the night, each one to be buried in the village of his birth.

No one from the crowd had remained.

In disbelief, perhaps in fear, each man, each woman, each child had silently turned away into the small streets that ran to the square, their trumpets, their drums, their screaming now silenced, their thoughts only of the creature they had seen and of the girl who had taken it into the fire.

It had been a trick, of course. No more. But still they had walked in silence.

"That was Leyla, wasn't it?" said Joaquim.

Denny nodded, her eyes still on the brightening skies.

"Yes."

"Then it is the second time your friend has saved you."

They turned, quickly. The shepherd stood behind them. The tall wooden stick in his hands, his words clear, his voice soft.

Slowly Joaquim and Denny rose to their feet, turning their backs to the sunrise, looking at the man they both had met. But had not known.

"So, you survived."

It wasn't a question. The shepherd seemed simply to be reminding them. Proving it to them.

"Which is more than he will have done."

The shepherd moved his stick towards the body of the monk, ruffling the cloth, lifting it to show the bones of the skeleton beneath, its yellowed skull buried in the angled, disjointed bones of its hands.

"When. . .?"

The words stuck in Joaquim's throat, his grip tightening on Denny, her body cold in the growing light of the day.

"His job was done," said the shepherd, slowly, letting the folds of the cloth fall once again into place. "His purpose served. He had waited a long time for the creature's return. And might be waiting yet, had it not been for the woman on the cliffs."

The wind blew gently through his long grey hair, bringing movement to the sides of his face, a face that otherwise remained quite still as the shepherd spoke.

"As she scattered the ashes of the fishing-girl, so she read out the words that would call up the spirit of the lobisomen. The creature's spirit was among those ashes. Now, once again, the creature was almost free."

"Isobel?"

Denny's word was soft, almost whispered. The shepherd nodded.

"The lobisomen took her body. But she needed you. To be completely free, the creature needed to take the soul of the only other woman in the family. You."

The shepherd tapped the dull grey paving-stones of the square with his stick. Gently. Looking down as he did so, as if lost in his own thoughts. His own memories.

"It was a mistake. Two burial urns. Two burials. So far apart."

The sun was climbing into the lower reaches of the skies, bringing with it the brilliant shades of red that reach across the mountains and flood the early morning skies of the Algarve.

The shepherd looked up again, the colours of the dawn washing across the deep furrows of his face. His brown eyes turned towards Denny.

"She might never have found you. Until, by chance, you visited the grave in the cathedral. And your friend called her with the words. And then died protecting you." The shepherd paused. "Had the lobisomen killed you there, she would have been free for ever. There would have been no *mordomos*. No monk. No fire." He nodded, still watching her. "Perhaps we should all be grateful to your friend."

Denny said nothing. She had been used as a trap. No more than carrion hung from a gibbet, to lure the creature from Hell that had wanted her soul. As he watched her, so the shepherd knew her thoughts.

"It was wrong. But the monk knew it was the only way."

Once again he looked away, watching the embers of the fire being blown slowly across the square.

"Who are you?" said Denny, at last, letting her words break the silence.

"It doesn't matter who I am. Or who I was. What matters is that they are now free. And that, at last, she is free with them."

"She?"

The shepherd looked up towards the skies, his eyes moving slowly across them, searching each corner of the blood-red heavens until they finally stopped, satisfied, at last, with what they saw.

"Elizabeth."

And slowly, Joaquim and Denny turned to face the sunrise. To see the broad, curling silhouettes of the birds as they climbed into the sky. Circling. And, with each broad sweep of the circle, moving higher and further from the land, balanced on the warm winds of the dawn.

The sequoia.

Slowly the birds moved through the skies. Dark tumbling shadows, caught in the first moments of the day, that seemed to drift towards the very edges of the world before turning and spinning silently towards the west.

In Spiritus.

Have you read ... ?

EVE'S PARTY

by Nick Turnbull

THE UNTOLD TERROR IS OUT ...

They called him the Seal Man.

Throughout the summer, he'd paddled along the edges of the South Devon coastline, his home-made canoe riding easily over the choppy, swirling surface of the sea. They said he lived in a caravan, somewhere behind Thurlestone Sands. Nobody really knew. Nor cared. Portlecombe was that kind of place.

Sometimes, as they left the harbour, heading for their lobster pots bobbling on the sea-bed off Start Point, the fishermen would wave, their shouts of "Hello!" drifting across the waves. The man would smile, then wave back, briefly.

This afternoon, there were no fishermen.

He'd felt the first sting of the rain as it had started to spit from the low, grey clouds. The waves were now higher, more frequent, their dark, tumbling bodies fringed with a white, bubbling spume that flicked across their edges. The pair of grey seals he had been watching had long since disappeared into one of the many caves that the centuries had hacked into the hard granite of the cliffs.

Glancing over his shoulder, he could now see the darkening front of the coming storm, moving in slowly but surely from the open sea. He knew he wouldn't have time to make it back to the sands. Five minutes. Perhaps ten, at the most, before it hit him. His canoe had begun to yaw from side to side as the wind freshened and the waves sharpened.

In front of him, the cliffs rose sheer from the water's edge, reaching high into the sky where their jagged crown scratched a crazy line across the tumbling clouds. The rain was now harsher, more insistent. He had to land.

With an increasing sense of urgency, his arms now began to work the paddle more viciously, the blades at either side of the canoe biting into the cold, broken valleys of the sea as the waves now ran towards the shoreline rocks, only finally to hurl themselves against the pitiless, ragged stone. It would be a losing battle. Hard as he might try, he could not outrun the storm. Nor could he fight the increasing strength of the waves that were now pushing him gradually but inevitably toward the boiling edges of the shore.

Desperately now, his eyes searched the rocks. He swung the canoe round so that it now faced the land. Running with the waves, the light vessel began to cut through the water, its sharp bow first burying itself in the waves, then rearing like a frightened mare into the spray that whipped across their surface.

It was a gamble. The man knew he had to land. Already filling with water as the rain began to hammer down from the heavy skies above, the frail canoe would not last long in seas that were now grown angry. He could only hope, as the land grew closer, to find a break in the rocks. Painfully, he clawed the paddle deep into the water at one side. The canoe turned, skidding across the wave-top, dropping back as the wave ploughed on, before then being picked up by the next as its dark, curling face loomed behind him.

With each wave, the shore grew nearer, louder. Still he could see no break. Thrown against the pitiless face of the rocks, he would shatter like a china plate hurled against the sides of a quarry. Around him, the waves now boiled, sensing perhaps that they were close to their final, headlong charge toward their own destruction.

There was no break. Only the relentless, deafening crash of the water breaking over the rocks, the howl of the wind and the scream of the gulls as they swooped and span through the sweeping curtains of rain. The canoe reared up, almost falling back upon itself. Desperately, the man threw himself forwards, stopping the boat's somersault. As he did so, he dropped the paddle and, lying in the water on the floor of the boat, he looked back into the steepling waves behind him and saw it briefly arc into the air, almost as if in goodbye, before disappearing into the spray.

The boat rocked violently as the waves now picked it up and threw it brutally from side to side. The man gripped its sides, staring up into the merciless rain, screaming and then silent, as if in final supplication for a death that would be quick.

Then he felt the wave lift him. Higher than before, the final throw of the dice. It seemed to the man that he was being hoisted high into Heaven. In the driving, howling rain, and surrounded by the screaming gulls, he seemed to perch on the crest of the wave for ever, as if already dead and now safely cradled in eternity. Until, with sickening violence, the boat was suddenly wrenched and thrown down against the greedy clutches of the rocks.

Buried in the centre of the explosion of sound that followed, the man knew little of what happened. He'd expected the sudden, searing agony of his body being broken against the cliff, dragged and splintered like a rag doll against the unforgiving, granite teeth. Instead, there had been nothing. A sharp crack on the side of his head and then silence.

And now, he lay, floating, his feet treading water in what seemed to be a pool. His head hurt. From somewhere, a soft, grey light filtered through the gloom, whilst outside, the waves continued to thunder and beat against the walls of the cave.

And then he realized.

The wave that had thrown him against the cliff, rather than hurling him to his death, had thrown him into one of the seal caves. A one in a million chance. Perhaps more. He put his hand to the side of his head. It had been bleeding. He must have hit it on the side of the entrance.

Slowly, his eyes grew used to the dim light of the

cave. Its roof was some ten or twelve feet above him, narrowing as it rose, its two sides meeting to form a line that ran back into the darker recesses of the cave. He kicked his feet and swam slowly towards the edge of the pool where a narrow path seemed to run along its side. Reaching it, he held on for a few moments and then carefully pulled himself up and out of the water. The noise he made echoed round the vaulted arches of the cave, a sharper sound now than the muffled threat of the seas beyond the cave's entrance.

He could see now that the cave stretched back far into the cliff. Oddly, there was no smell. No seals had used this cave. Nor any other animal.

He stood up, the heavy sea water falling from his clothes and dripping on to the stone beneath his feet. In the half-light, he began to edge forwards, at first with very short, careful steps. At his side, the waters of the pool were calm, a slight swell prompted only by the flurry of water at the cave's entrance. The pool seemed dark. It was almost certainly deep.

His breathing was heavy, painful. As he moved further into the cave, so the light began to falter. He stopped, wondering why he was walking away from the sea. The storm would subside. In time, the waves would calm and he would be safe to leave and somehow scramble along the shoreline to safety. And yet, he was walking on, almost as if he had been asked to. Almost as if he was the first man ever to have found this dark chamber and almost as if the spirits of time and therefore of the earth, needed to talk with him.

With his right hand, he felt his way along the wall. Still the stone path ran before him, a natural feature carved and modelled by the centuries. If anything, it seemed now to be growing wider. It was almost exactly where it widened sufficiently to become something of a platform that the man found it, hanging from a rusting nail hammered into the rock.

A small candle-lantern. A metal cage, dirty glass. The kind of lantern once in common use. Many years before.

The man stared at it, disbelieving at first. Then, slowly, almost as if expecting it to crumble in his hands, he reached up and took it carefully off the nail. He brought it down, his gaze running over the lamp's simple, almost crude, design. He turned it round. There was still a candle inside.

At its back, he found a small leather pouch hanging from the metal frame. He stooped, putting the lamp on the ground and then held the pouch closer to his face, studying it closely. At its neck, there was a short piece of string which snapped when he pulled at it. He let the pieces fall to the ground. Still the water echoed round the cave as it continued to fall from his clothes.

The pouch opened. Inside were several long, thin

wooden sticks, darkened at one end. The man was puzzled and then realized what he was holding. Whoever had left the lamp here had left some matches with it.

He took one out and, bending down to the lamp again, he looked carefully at each of its sides until he found the glass panel that would slide out to allow access to the candle. He found it. He felt the candle. It was dry.

The first match broke as he scratched it along the dry stone of the cave wall. So did the second. The third, however, sputtered into life and burnt for long enough to allow the man to push it slowly into the lamp and put it to the candle. It was a small flame at first but then, as the wax began to melt and the taper became more exposed, so the flame grew.

He straightened up, holding the lamp aloft. Now he could see deep into the cave, the light of the candle revealing that the path widened as it led to a small, high-ceilinged chamber. The waters of the pool splashed gently at its side. Slowly, he walked forwards again, his attention now taken by what seemed to be a stone box, laid on the floor of the chamber. The shadows thrown by the light of the lamp flickered along the walls as he moved. He stopped and listened. The sound of the seas outside had gone. Even the movement of the pool was silent. There was only the fall of water from his clothes. He coughed, letting the echoes die before moving once more towards the box.

He could see now that it was in two halves, the upper half acting as a lid. He thought it to be some five feet in length. Perhaps no more than two in height. He knelt beside it, putting the lamp on the ground where the light burned perfectly still. Deep in the cave, the air did not move.

There was no indication on the box of what it might be. It was man-made. That much was clear, for carved across its top was what appeared to be a snake. Other than that, it was featureless. The dust that had settled on it suggested that it had been where it was for a very long time. Like the lamp, thought the man.

He reached out to it, putting his hands at either side of the lid. Hesitating briefly, he then tried to move it, testing its weight. To his surprise, it seemed to move easily. Afraid of damaging it, however, he worked carefully, edging the lid off, inch by inch.

As he did so, he thought it odd that the candle flame had begun to flicker. Perhaps the air did move down here after all.

It took him some minutes before he was satisfied that he had moved it sufficiently to lift the lantern and look inside the stone box.

He stood up, picking up the lamp. The side of his head had begun to bleed again.

He slowly moved the light across to the box and,

as he looked now at what was in it, the horror of the storm, the rocks, the sense of sudden death, paled beside the sight of a small girl lying in a stone coffin, her arms across her chest, her eyes closed. He gasped for breath, his heart hammering fast against his ribs.

"I don't…"

The girl's body twitched. Her hands moved, unfolding from their clasp.

The man didn't move, frozen by the sight of the child whose head now turned towards him, whose eyes slowly opened and whose white lips began to smile.

"Thank you."

Falling backwards, dropping the lantern, screaming, he turned to run and, thrashing in the air, found himself falling into the dark waters of the pool. As his head broke the surface, he was briefly aware of the creature, its black glistening head now towering above him, risen from the depths of the water and now breaking open its jaws to sink them about his head and drag him kicking, struggling and finally limp to the lower layers of the pool.

"What do you think happened, Grandad?"

Lindsay looked across the kitchen towards the windows where the old man was standing, gazing out impassively over the small Portlecombe harbour.

"Drowned," he said, after a few moments. "His own fault."

He spoke with a soft, Devon burr. Tom Walker had been born in Portlecombe and had lived there for most of his seventy-two years. Once, he'd been a fisherman but now, the nearest he came to a boat was to sit on the quayside, spinning stories with the other old men of the village.

"What do you mean? His fault?"

"Just what I said." Her grandfather turned from the window. "If you go fiddling about in a boat that size and then expect to get away with it when it starts blowing a force nine, then you'll get all that's coming to you."

"That's not very kind."

"Maybe not. But I've seen plenty of fools like him and they all end up the same way."

Lindsay stood up and began to tidy what was left of breakfast from the kitchen table.

"All he wanted to do was watch the seals."

"Well, he'll be watching them with St Peter now."

The lifeboat had spent two days searching the coastline for the Seal Man. Without success. They'd found a splintered paddle on one of the beaches which they assumed must have been his. They'd also found what was left of his boat, floating, partially submerged, some two hundred metres from the shore. If it had been smashed on the rocks, the waves must have dragged it back out to sea. Of the Seal Man himself, there had been no sign.

"I'm going off with Ben this morning," said Lindsay, turning on the taps at the kitchen sink. "He says he knows where there's some ruins I could use."

"Ruins?"

"For my project."

"Ah, yes."

Tom Walker remembered Lindsay saying something about a school project. He hadn't been entirely sure of what a "photographic essay" might be but it sounded important. He glanced out of the window, his eyes scanning the deep blue sky.

"Well, you'll have a good day for it."

"Is it OK with you?"

Her grandfather smiled.

"I don't mind. You go if you want to. I've just got a little shopping to do."

It was Lindsay's turn to smile. She knew perfectly well that her grandfather's "shopping" meant buying a loaf of bread and then nipping smartly into the Victoria Inn.

At fifteen, Ben Carson was two years older than Lindsay. Tall, with a shock of thick blonde hair and calm grey eyes, he was going to be a pilot. One day. Right now, he was just happy growing up in Portlecombe.

Lindsay had run into Ben, quite literally, during

her first visit to the small town the year before. Chasing after her grandfather, who'd somehow managed to leave the cottage with both sets of door keys, she'd hurtled round a street corner only to collide with the unsuspecting boy. Neither of them had been hurt. The only damage done was to the box of eggs that Ben had been carrying and it had been an unlikely start to a friendship that had lasted through-out that summer and one which they had both been very happy to renew every holiday since then.

Ben didn't know too much about Lindsay's background. Only that she came from the North. That she went away to school. That her parents had split up. That she now spent most of her holidays with her grandfather, old Tom Walker.

He was standing on the quayside when Lindsay appeared. Below him, his brother's fishing boat was moored to the wooden landing steps that led down to the water. The tide was high.

"Morning."

"Changed your mind?"

Lindsay nodded towards the boat as she walked up to him.

"About what?" said Ben.

"Helping Dan."

"No, he's fine. And anyway, Ahab's going with him."

As he spoke, he saw his brother appear at the far

side of the small harbour-side car-park, followed by a shorter man with a thick ginger beard.

"Is he really called Ahab?" said Lindsay.

"As far as I know."

"Wasn't that the man who went off chasing Moby Dick?"

"Don't think so," said Ben. "I don't think he's that old."

Dan Carson was older and taller than his brother. Several years of working the crabbing boats had thickened his neck and arms and, since he was rarely seen without stubble on his chin, he was known locally as 'Desperate'. His smile was broad and his skin tanned by the long summer days spent on the water.

"Hi, Ben. Lindsay."

"Hi, Dan."

"You want to change your mind about coming?"

Ahab had already gone down the steps to the boat and had disappeared into the small cabin that housed the steering wheel and provided simple shelter when the weather turned sour.

"Not today," said Ben. "Lindsay wants to take some photographs of bricks."

"Sounds fun."

Lindsay smiled at Dan. "Ruins. And it's for a school project."

"Even more fun."

Below them, the boat's engine suddenly burst

into life, roaring briefly as Ahab pulled the throttle back before allowing it to settle into its more familiar muffled pulse.

"Sounds like Ahab's in a hurry. Tell your grandad I was asking after him, Linds."

"I will."

She knew the Carsons and Walkers went back a long way.

Dan threw his duffel bag down on to the wide, curving deck of the Portlecombe "crabber" below him, where Ahab was now untying the ropes that held it to the harbour wall. He paused as he walked down the wooden steps to the boat.

"Have a good time with the bricks."

Moments later, the crabber was weaving its way carefully through the various boats that lay at anchor in the harbour. Ben watched it go and then turned to Lindsay.

"It's a long walk."

"Doesn't matter. The sun's shining."

Once clear of the harbour, Ahab now headed down the short estuary that led to the open sea beyond. On the beach to his left, he could see children playing at the edges of the water, others playing in the sand, their parents sitting beneath brightly coloured umbrellas. A flash of red amongst the rocks at one side caught his eye. Someone was standing there. A small girl. She seemed to be watching them go by.

"Ahab!"

Dan was shouting from the front of the boat, where he had been oiling the winch that would soon be hauling the crab pots up from the sea floor.

"Mind that boat!"

His attention taken by the beach, Ahab hadn't noticed the small sailing boat that was now heading straight for them. He pulled quickly on the lever to his right, throwing the boat into reverse and slowing it, allowing the small dinghy to pass by in front.

"You missed them!" shouted Dan, smiling.

Ahab stuck his head out of the wheelhouse window, a broad grin on his face.

"Just practisin'."

Dan watched the small boat sail by, keeling slightly in the breeze. There were two people in it. One waved. He waved back, listening to the growl of the diesel engine as the fishing boat once more moved forwards, picking up speed. He wondered if they'd noticed the shark's fin cutting through the water some fifty yards behind them.

"There's been a few of them about this summer," he said, walking back to join Ahab.

"Just a basking shark," said Ahab. "Won't hurt nobody." He swung the wheel gently to his left.

As the boat drew closer, the fish disappeared beneath the surface of the water. Ahab slowed and then finally cut the engine, allowing the boat to drift. Leaning over the side of the boat, they could clearly see the dark shadow of the creature swimming slowly below them.

"It's big," said Ahab.

He started the engine again, heading for the Greystone Rocks that marked the entrance to the estuary. Once safely past them, Ahab opened the throttle to full speed as the boat now moved into the open sea.

As they did so, unseen, the fish behind them had now turned and was following.

It took them almost an hour to walk to Lindsay's 'pile of bricks'. In the heat of the morning sun it had been hard work, and by the time they reached the old gates that sat at the top of the driveway, they were both grateful for the two bottles of water Ben had been carrying in his shoulderbag.

"Is this it?" said Lindsay, sitting on the ground and leaning back against one of the peeling gateposts.

"No. These are just the gates."

Lindsay smiled.

"OK."

Ben pointed beyond the gates. Thick overhead with the branches of trees that had grown and become entangled, a muddy track led downhill, curling finally to the left and disappearing behind a group of tall pine trees.

"There's not much of it left," said Ben. "I

mean, I don't know what sort of ruins you're looking for."

"Any old ruins," said Lindsay. "Preferably with a ghost."

Ben laughed.

"I don't think they come out in the daytime."

Finishing their water, they started walking down the sloping driveway. As they walked, so it felt cooler. The trees above blocked the sunlight. A breeze seemed to blow up towards them. After the heat of the earlier walk, it was refreshing.

"What happened to it?" said Lindsay.

"It burnt down," said Ben.

"When?"

"Oh, I don't know. Years ago."

"And they never tried to rebuild it?"

"No. To be honest, I don't think many people even know it's here. You'll never hear anybody talk about it in the village."

They had reached the pines.

The sea was calm. Almost flat. In the distance, they could see the short stubby flags floating on the surface that told where the first string of pots were lying. Some two miles out from the shore, they were alone, the only sound – apart from the steady rhythm of the Perkins diesel beneath the deck – being the occasional gull's cry as the birds circled high above.

The flags were nearer now. Ahab slowed the engine.

"Fingers crossed," said Dan, walking forwards towards the winch.

It hadn't been a good year for the Portlecombe fishermen and Dan had almost become used to pulling up a string of a dozen pots, only to find nothing in them.

Ahab waited until the flags were no more than ten or twelve metres away and then cut the engine, letting the boat drift slowly in towards them. Leaning over the side of the boat, Dan had a long metal hook in his hands which, as they drew alongside the first flag, he swung into the water, catching the rope that dropped down towards the seabed from the base of the flag. Pulling it up, he looped it over the drum of the winch and fastened it to the hoop which was bolted into the wooden planking of the deck. Turning the handle on the side of the winch, he then wound in the initial slack of the line that disappeared down into the depths of the ocean, until, as it tightened, contact was made with the first pot.

Ahab had left the small wheelhouse and was standing on the deck, gazing out over the flat sea. The wind had died away. Dan had started the small electric winch-motor which was now humming quietly as the pots were slowly pulled to the surface. The heat from the sun was fierce. In the distance, where the shoreline should have been, a haze had settled, turning the line of cliffs into a narrow, smudged margin at the bottom of the sky. The boat rocked slightly, shaken by the movement of the pots on the other end of the line.

Ahab found himself watching the surface of the sea some thirty yards to his left. There, a small cormorant was floating on the water, paddling lazily, dipping its head every so often, as if drinking. The bird was also suffering from the heat.

The dorsal fin appeared first, followed quickly by the smaller tail fin, as the fish came to the surface. Surprised, the cormorant shook its wings and with a short cry, lifted itself into the air, flying quickly away to the south. Ahab watched as the two fins slowly cut through the water. Looking at the distance between them, he thought the shark was probably some fifteen feet long. And it wasn't a basking shark.

"Dan."

"Yeah?"

Dan looked across the boat.

"Have a look at this."

"What?"

"Over there. In the water."

Ahab pointed to the fins which were now beginning a wide circle around the boat.

"What is it?"

"I think it's a mako," said Ahab. "But I've never seen one that size."

As he spoke, the two fins slowly sank back beneath the surface and the fish was gone.

They turned the bend by the pine trees and then stopped. At first neither of them spoke. In front of them, now almost entirely overgrown with ivy; with grasses; with brambles, were the crumbling, broken walls of what had obviously once been a large house.

The roof had long gone, charred stumps of timber being all that remained of its rafters. The windows were no more than holes in the walls. Where the large front doors had once hung, there was now simply a wide opening through which the decaying interior of the house could be glimpsed.

Standing quietly, almost peacefully, in the sunlight, it reminded Lindsay of a doll's house, whose childish owner had thrown a tantrum, stamped on it and left it to rot at the bottom of the garden.

"I told you there wasn't much left of it," said Ben, as they started walking again.

"It's fine," said Lindsay, taking her camera out of its leather case. "And it looks really weird."

"Is that good?"

"Absolutely."

She stopped, lifting her camera up to her eye and pointing it at the house. The shutter clicked. She smiled.

"You know, it's odd," she said, "but if you listen

carefully, it's almost as if you can hear the sounds of children playing."

As they walked up to the house, Lindsay took more photographs. The slight breeze had died and the sun was now high, bathing the ruins in a harsh, glaring light. But it was only as they began to walk round to the side of the house, following the track of what had once been a garden path, that Ben realized what was wrong.

"Linds."

"Yeah?"

"Have you noticed something?"

"Like what?"

"The sun's shining. Right?"

"Right."

"So why does it feel so cold?"